Acclaim for Nora Gallagher's

CHANGING LIGHT

"Gallagher beautifully captures the fears and ideals of the scientists who spoke out against the monster they had created."

—*Los Angeles* magazine

"An elegantly written, deeply intelligent, literary romance."

—*San Francisco Chronicle*

"An elegant and graceful book about three people caught, knowingly or by accident, in the vortex of that deadly undertaking [at Los Alamos]. . . . A redemptive love story of considerable tenderness."

—*Santa Barbara News-Press*

"At once a love story, a thriller, and a reflection on the demands of conscience. And it is a wonderful read. Gallagher's prose is always elegant and sinuous, but it never calls attention to itself. As with Flaubert, we know ourselves to be in the presence of a shaping artistic presence, but that presence never intrudes upon the action or the characters. An exceptional work of fiction."

—*Anglican Theological Review*

"Known for reporting on ordinary people in extraordinary times, Gallagher focuses here on outright extraordinary people."

—*More* magazine

"Gallagher evokes both the secrecy of the Manhattan Project and the agony of new love with the sureness of a seasoned fiction veteran."

—*The Regal Courier* (Oregon)

"This is a spare, beautifully crafted story about people trying to sort right from wrong when time has run out and moral certainty becomes impossible. Gallagher's characters, like all of us at one time or another, must somehow choose and live with the consequences. She has given us a jewel of a novel."

—Mark Salzman, author of *Lying Awake*

"At last, a novel about something. Nora Gallagher captures with dazzling beauty the lives of a woman and a man caught in the grip of history and our country's shadowed past. I held my breath reading it." —Annie Dillard, author of *Pilgrim at Tinker Creek*

"*Changing Light* is a lyrical and passionate novel that takes on some of the largest matters of our day with no loss to its intimacy. Conviction that writing matters the way life matters is Gallagher's hallmark." —Thomas McGuane, author of *Gallatin Canyon*

"An incredibly beautiful story with echoes of Ondaatje and McEwan. Haunting and unforgettable, this is a smashing fiction debut from one of our most thoughtful writers."

—Martha Sherrill, author of *The Ruins of California*

Nora Gallagher

CHANGING LIGHT

Nora Gallagher is the author of *Things Seen and Unseen: A Year Lived in Faith* and *Practicing Resurrection: A Memoir of Work, Doubt, Discernment, and Moments of Grace.* Her essays, book reviews, and journalism have appeared in *The New York Times Magazine*, *The Washington Post*, *DoubleTake*, and *Mother Jones*, among other publications. She is also the editor of the award-winning *Notes from the Field*, a collection of literary essays about the outdoors. She grew up in New Mexico and lives with her husband in California and New York City.

CHANGING

LIGHT

CHANGING

LIGHT

Nora Gallagher

Vintage Contemporaries
Vintage Books
A Division of Random House, Inc.
New York

FIRST VINTAGE CONTEMPORARIES EDITION, FEBRUARY 2008

The Library of Congress has cataloged the Pantheon edition as follows:
Gallagher, Nora, [date]
Changing light / Nora Gallagher.
p. cm.
1. Scientists—Fiction. 2. Women painters—Fiction. 3. Manhattan Project (U.S.)—
Fiction. 4. Los Alamos Scientific Laboratory—Fiction. 5. Los Alamos (N.M.)—Fiction.
6. Atomic Bomb—United States—History—Fiction. I. Title.
PS3607.A415442C47 2006
813'.54—dc22
2006020134

Vintage ISBN: 978-0-307-27755-8

Book design by Wesley Gott

www.vintagebooks.com

Printed in the United States of America
10 9 8 7 6 5 4 3 2 1

For Vincent Stanley

ONE

Eleanor stood up in the garden from tilling a plot for early let-tuce, shook off her hands, and stuffed them into the sleeves of her brown wool sweater. The wind was up; it blew dirt from the adobe wall into the newly hoed ground, dry pods from the chamisa bushes rattled like bones. She walked toward the house, sniffing the air like the dog beside her, climbed the steps to the door, opened it, walked past the stove, her hands still nestled in the sleeves—like one of those Chinamen, she thought to herself—and turned into the bedroom, where she'd put him last night.

All night long he'd listed between sleep and a rushing wakefulness, muttering in what she thought was German but couldn't be sure. "Lotte," he cried. *"Raus aus dem Feuer!"* And then, a word she thought must be English but didn't know. "Implosion," he said. She had placed rags on his head soaked in water and chamisa to break his fever, get him to sweat. He looked to her like men she'd met in New York: dark, Jewish, probably; curly black hair. Last night, when she'd found him lying in the *bosque* beside the river, his face was turned toward the sky. The dog circled him. She bent over him, her heart beating in her throat. His lips were cracked, his eyes shut. His wet khaki pants clung to his legs like vines. He grasped a pair of boots by their laces and a heavy belt in his right hand. Her eyes moved from the boots to the river and the mesa that rose up on the other side.

She bent down. "Hello?" she said. "Hello." His head moved, the eyelids lifted. His eyes were a pale, startling blue. "Lotte?" he said.

"No," she replied. His accent on the name was thick, and in her memory she heard someone's voice speaking with these inflections, like an echo off a high stone wall. "Are you ill?" "Ill," he repeated, and ran his tongue over his lips. She walked back through thick sand to the Ford, took her canteen out of the glove box, returned. He drank in small gulps, like a bird; she could see the water traveling down his throat. Water spilled out of his mouth and onto his chest, and he shivered. She jerked the canteen away.

"Can you walk?"

She wrapped his head in her father's old sweater, the sleeves crossed over his eyes. She stood between his legs, grasped his ankles, and pulled. When she got him to the Ford, she squatted down, put her arms under his shoulders, and heaved him up to sitting against the front tire, then pulled him forward, whispering to him as she would to a horse, "Easy, now, easy, don't fall."

She had planned to drive him straight to the hospital, but as she started the engine he whispered to her, "No doctors." She looked over at him and saw in his face a barely controlled desperation. And so she took him home. She shouldered him into the house as she had her brother when he came home drunk from a debutante's party, and tipped him into bed.

She stood over him in the room plastered white with thick adobe walls that she and Estaban built last May before the sudden rain came in July and washed all the plaster off the outer walls and the dirt out of her garden, leaving only gravel, and she had to dig her carrots up with a pick.

He whispered in his sleep, half wakeful. His eyes opened and he saw her arm pass over his body like the shadow of a bird.

"What happened to you?" she asked. Leo turned his head to the wall, licking his lips.

We tickled the dragon's tail, Leo thought. One of us was burned.

Slotin was moving the two half-moons together with screwdrivers. The counter ticked and the red signal lamps were blinking. The lamps blinked faster as Slotin moved the half spheres closer, like a drummer or a Japanese man with his chopsticks.

Then there was the sound of a screwdriver hitting the floor. The meter stopped. Leo heard the silence first. He yelled to Slotin, "*Raus aus dem Feuer!*"

The moon had pulled him across the deserted streets, between the trees, to the hole in the fence that the teenagers made to outfox the guards. His legs felt like sacks filled with sand. He got down on his hands and knees and bowed his head, feeling along the sharp ends of the linked fence with his hands first before he pushed himself through. He sat on the other side, his breath hot in his lungs, and then started to weep, his whole body shuddering. To be free of the place. He pulled the knapsack stuffed with a blanket and bread and cheese through the fence after him, adjusted the heavy belt stuffed with money that he carried with him through all border crossings, stood up, and began to find his way. In the dark were animal shapes moving through the trees: a deer, then a wild turkey, its wings folded neatly against its round breast. After a while he noticed the small swift bats flying past his nose, sonar alerting them to his head. He felt a sudden calm to be among them, the life of the world; as a boy he had always loved the dark.

Leo could not stay awake. He felt he should; he did not even know where he was or who this woman was who bent over him, asking questions. But he was too full of dreams or memories, he was not sure which. Slotin's hands. The Chicago beehive assembly. His sister, Lotte, standing in the Woodrow Wilson train station in Prague.

Eleanor washed red and white beans in a colander at the sink. She poured water from a large earthenware pitcher through the beans and watched their colors darken as the liquid ran over and through them. She caught a cup of water from under the colander and poured it on the pink geraniums in the Folgers can on the windowsill. Outside the light changed to pink; streaks of purple lit up the Jemez. Her garden looked red for an instant. Tomorrow, the doctor, she thought, and almost said it out loud. Tomorrow she would drive into town. Even the unconventional *gringa* can't allow a strange man to stay in her house, even if he's ill.

She checked on him but he was deep in sleep, so she lit her kerosene reading lamp, but didn't sit down. She was reading Willa Cather, a sweet, sad story about a family of Bohemians in Nebraska. She turned on the radio to hear a little jazz and felt lonely for the first time in months, when, for the first time in months, there was someone else in the house.

Her living room had a little fireplace placed in the wall at waist level that Griefa and Estaban built one afternoon.

"Ande yo caliente ya riase la gente," Estaban said when he was finished, and when Eleanor asked him *"En inglés?"* he shrugged his shoulders. Griefa said, "As long as I am warm, let the people laugh." Griefa had plastered the walls wearing a dress—her bra showing under the arms—and a hat with plastic flowers. The floors were dirt mixed with cow's blood, made by the dancers at San Ildefonso Pueblo. It had aged to a shiny deep red. Beside the bed was a wool rug in gray and black from the Ortega family in Chimayo. Against the wall were several canvases, and Eleanor's paints were neatly lined

up. The ceiling was made of heavy *vigas* with *latias* woven between them, thin aspen saplings that Estaban had cut in the forest above the boy's school at Los Alamos.

This was what she had wanted, this room, imagining it while lying in the apartment in New York, sick with a headache, unable to go outside and face the crowded streets for fear of the paralyzing din in her head. She had built this house room by room in her mind ever since she had first seen New Mexico and known she would have to come back. When she and Griefa and Estaban were done, the three of them had breathed in the smell of damp plaster and then sat on the *portal* outside and drunk Coors beer and eaten some green chile stew Griefa had made and looked out at the blue Jemez Mountains.

Leo opened his eyes and looked up at the ceiling. How many days? One? Two? Whose room is this?

The light entered the room at quarter past six; his Timex was still ticking. He turned in the bed to watch the door, to wait until she was awake. He had not fully seen her, just her looming face over his, her hands near his mouth, her arm over his head. The sleeve of her white shirt. As she came through the door, he blinked as if to take a photograph. Woman walking through a doorway. White shirt, black skirt. A pensive face, fair skin, shadows under her eyes. Not a trace of rouge. Her hair was dark and straight, cut in a bob; she pushed it back with her left hand. White hands, thin wrists. She obscured and absorbed light as she entered. Leo thought of how neutrons slowing in the body's watery cells scattered damage.

She leaned over him.

"Is this your house?" Leo asked.

She jumped back; her feet made the floor speak. He smiled.

She stayed where she was, watchful. He tried to broaden his smile, to appear innocent. Who was she?

"It is."

"It's very nice." Then, "I'm hungry. I'm sorry to trouble you."

She turned and left the room, returning with a bowl of chicken broth and a hard-boiled egg. She spooned the broth into his mouth. She tapped the egg against the wall above his shoulder and peeled the shell into pieces, which fell onto a blue damask napkin she had laid on the bed. She split the egg expertly with her thumbs and popped half into his mouth. He licked the dry, powdery yolk and the smooth white and swallowed. Then closed his eyes. She wiped her hands on her skirt, took the bowl from the side of the bed, and stood up. For a second she lost her balance and pressed her palm against the wall.

Memories called on Leo, plucked at his sleeve. The past was everywhere. A chain of laboratories, from the old world to the new, his life of the last thirteen years, now broken, disrupted: Berlin, the Cavendish lab in Cambridge, Chicago; then here, the Project. The organizing principles: war and flight relieved by discovery.

He had taken the train from Cambridge through the gloomy English countryside into London, that sad city with its piles of rubble. He could hear the ticking of his heart on the long ocean crossing when they neared the places where the German subs might lie under the ship's weight. Beside the docks when they disembarked in New York there was a mound of oranges lit by flares.

They were the first oranges he'd seen in four years. He reached for one, feeling like a schoolboy, and the beauty of the city broke all around him. He would look back on that in the years to come as one of the last moments of Before, followed by After.

He found a hotel next to a good drugstore with a counter at which he could order scrambled eggs with matzo. He wished simply to walk in the great city of New York again, to breathe in its smell of subway and taxi exhaust and cooking and garbage, to listen to the conversations on the street, to be in a place free of the dread the war had brought to Europe, but he had work to do. The next day, he took a cab downtown and met Wigner at his Greenwich Village walk-up that smelled of cooked cabbage. Wigner, still yellow from a bout of jaundice, wore a suit complete with a vest even on that hot July day. Neither one of them knew exactly where Einstein was staying; it was a rented summer house out on Nassau Point. Leo had been Einstein's student in Berlin, and had an idea to explain to him, and once, years ago, in a more innocent time, the two of them had patented together a refrigerator that ran on gas: these were his credentials. Leo had never owned a car and could not drive. Once they reached Long Island, Wigner drove in circles until, exasperated, Leo told him to stop. A small boy stood beside the road, fooling with a fishing pole. Leo leaned out the window and gave it a shot. Did he know where Professor Einstein was living? He did.

"I thought he might be a real American celebrity," Leo said.

Wigner, already tired of Leo's ego, was silent.

The boy trotted ahead of the sedan and Wigner drove with care.

Einstein was sitting on a small screened-in porch crowded with old summer cottage furniture: wicker chairs with flaking white paint, a table with a water glass on it, an old canvas deck chair, three croquet mallets leaning against a wall in the corner. The floorboards had been painted white. The water of the sound could be seen through the grid of the screens. He was as Leo remembered him: a huge head, furrowed forehead, wisps of white hair, deep brown playful eyes. An English writer had said he looked like a reliable watchmaker in a small town who might have collected butterflies on a Sunday.

He wore a pair of old khakis, fraying at the cuffs, and deck shoes. His eyes looked at Leo as they had when he was his student in Berlin, asking him why had he come, what did he want?

Someone brought in trays of sandwiches: cheese and cucumber.

Einstein smoked his pipe, didn't eat much. They drank nothing but seltzer and spoke only in German. It was so much like summer afternoons in Prague, Leo grew homesick.

"When we left Caputh in 'thirty-two, you remember, the house Elsa loved in the country," Einstein was saying, "I told her, 'Turn around. You will never see it again.' "

Leo nodded, remembering his mother's tea roses, Fermi's goldfish pond in Rome, and Lotte, always Lotte, the last time he saw her, running toward him so fast, he had to pull the cigar out of his mouth before she hit his chest. "In the lab, I am turning salt to blue air!" she had said. She smelled like their mother. He breathed in his family. Now each of them—the roses, the goldfish, his sister, his memories—under boots, in a camp.

Wigner, impatient, leaned forward, his hands on his knees. Leo noticed he had a smudge on his shirt. He looked at Leo.

"Go ahead," he said. "Tell him about your great idea."

"Secondary neutron experiments," Leo began. And, finally, "Chain reaction in uranium and graphite."

"*Daran habe ich gar nicht gedacht,*" Einstein said, with astonishment and, to Leo's surprise, evident pleasure.

He asked Leo a lot of questions, but the implications were already clear to him.

"If I have thought of this, so might our counterparts in Germany," Leo said.

Einstein nodded quickly.

Leo told him of his private fund-raising efforts, and his realization that they must enlist the riches of governments. If it was possible, could Einstein write to Queen Elizabeth? President Roosevelt?

"Just to get started," Leo said, "I need to buy some graphite."

"But it may not work," Wigner interjected. "He could be wrong. We would make fools of ourselves."

Einstein looked at Wigner and smiled. Leo realized he was above the fear of being a fool—a true American celebrity.

On the way home, Leo laughed out loud. Wigner frowned.

"You're distracting me from driving," he said.

"He liked it that he had never thought of it," Leo said. "What a relief it must be to him *not* to have thought of something."

There was a turf war over who would build the experimental lab; the University of Chicago won. Not knowing what amount of radiation might be released, Fermi and Leo found a doubles squash court under the football field stands, a place underground. They worked with graphite bricks, and after a while they looked like coal miners, their lab coats smudged and sooted, their faces darkened like minstrels. The guards at the doors shivered in the cold until they dressed themselves in raccoon coats found in an abandoned locker.

Early December. Bitter cold. That morning, they had received word that two million Jews had died in Europe. Leo and Fermi entered the squash court that held the pile. Covered in a black balloon cloth, it looked like a giant beehive. They began removing the rods one by one. The last one came out only in the most careful increments. Fermi was at work on his slide rule. As the rod was moved out, the scalers clicked faster, then subsided. Fermi smiled. The balcony above the court now held more than twenty men standing in coats and gloves, physicists, mainly, who had helped them with the work. Arthur Compton, the photon master, came down and stood next to Fermi. At eleven-thirty Fermi said, "I'm hungry. Let's go to lunch."

It was an Italian lunch. They didn't come back until two. More men packed the balcony. Fermi ordered the control rod to be pulled out twelve inches. The counters began to click so fast, the sound became a roar. At that point, Fermi ordered that they switch from the counters to a chart recorder. In the abrupt silence, everyone watched the recorder's pen as it rose and rose across the measuring paper, a line shooting ever upward. The hair stood up on the back of Leo's head.

Suddenly, Fermi lifted his hand. "The pile has gone critical," he said.

Two minutes went by. The neutron intensity doubled. Leo saw a bead of sweat form on Compton's forehead as he leaned toward Fermi. How long was he going to let it go? Leo knew exactly how quickly it could run away. Melt down. Kill them all. The stuff of nightmares. But Fermi looked calm. He waited. Four and a half minutes went by.

"ZIP in!" he said, and the men pushed the rods back in. A kind of sigh went out, and the fear in the balcony lifted and was gone.

Wigner produced the Chianti he had bought months earlier, before Italian wine was no longer possible to buy, and they all sipped a little out of paper cups. Compton said he was going to call James Conant, their new liaison to the White House. They had worked out a funny little code, and he came back to tell them what they'd said.

"Jim," Compton had said to Conant, "the Italian navigator has just landed in the New World."

"Is that so!" Conant had replied. "Were the natives friendly?"

"Everyone landed safe and happy."

The men laughed, and Wigner slapped Compton on the back, and then, one by one, they wandered out into the winter night, leaving Fermi and Leo alone. Everyone had signed the bottle's straw wrapping except the two of them.

"I can't tell what this day will be called," Leo said to Fermi. "The day the earth stood still at our bravado, or the blackest day in the history of mankind."

Fermi, that smiling Italian, nodded his head.

· · ·

Eleanor took off her moccasins, put on her boots, and walked outside. The cold air struck her face. As she walked out to the little blue gate, she thought about whether he was a bank robber. She opened the gate, closed it behind her. The gray and black dog, Rita, followed at her heels; she had found her as a puppy in a yard in Taos, tied to a tree, her ribs like barrel staves. Eleanor had offered fifty cents for her on the spot and held her on her lap all the way home. As she and the dog walked down the path, Eleanor looked once over her shoulder at the Sangre de Cristos, which still had snow on them at the top, the snow on the aspen trees making an outline of a horse's head. In front of her, the ground sloped down toward the arroyo. Juniper trees with bark like old skin, furrowed and pockmarked, and small gray berries. Pinions between them, smaller.

She heard a deep croaking sound and looked up. When she had walked out on this land for the first time, she had heard that sound and looked at her feet for a frog—midwestern girl. But then she realized the croaking came from a tree. A frog caught in a tree? She imagined a frog tethered to the trunk of a pinion, drying out in the sun. Then she saw the raven sitting on a branch; he pumped his chest and sounded like a bullfrog. She laughed at him then, imitator of frogs. Now the raven flapped his wings in the juniper to her left, croaked, and moved into the sky. Rita pointed her nose at him, let the wind flatten her ears. At the edge of the arroyo, a gourd plant had left its dry tendrils stretched out along the bank like lace. Rabbit burrows left deep round o's in the arroyo's side. As Eleanor stepped across a thin gravel streambed, now dried many months, she looked down and saw the edge of something different from a rock. She bent over and lifted it gently out of the sand. A shard of pottery, its shape almost square, the top longer than the bottom. It fit perfectly in her palm. It was gray with black stripes; the stripes moved across the gray surface in a diagonal line. One line grew thick and formed a triangle. She stared at it. Its weight was nothing. She had never found anything like it before. She turned it over in her palm; she wondered how old it was, what kind of pot it had come from, and whether she might be able to paint something like it. Had they lived here, on what was now her land, or had it been simply dropped by a woman on her way south? She looked through the trees toward the city. What was here then? Where were they going? She wrapped the shard in her white lace handkerchief and tucked it in the pocket of her man's shirt.

Once the experiment in Chicago demonstrated that his theory of chain reaction was workable, Leo knew that it was only a matter of time. The letter arrived at his Chicago hotel in the spring. He was needed, Robert Oppenheimer said, for a lengthy "physics conference" in the western United States.

He sent his reply and packed his suitcases. As he walked toward the train station, two men came up on either side of him. "Mr. Simms?" one of them said, the one wearing a tan Bogart hat. Leo didn't reply. "Mr. Simms," he said again, a hand on Leo's arm. Leo remembered his new name. "I am he."

He was given a ticket by the man in the red tie standing near the water fountain at the station. He read of his destination as he walked toward the tracks: Lamy, New Mexico. The note continued, "Go to 109 East Palace Street, Santa Fe, New Mexico. There you will find how to complete your trip." When he found his Pullman room, he put away his suitcase and read his old name printed on it for all to see. A long ride out, through cornfields and plains to the little mud train station with the red tile roof that reminded him vaguely of Fiesole, the mud saloon next door, the long treeless plain, and the queer car ride to Santa Fe with the dark Spanish man who did not speak to him. He was dropped off with his bags at a low string of buildings near the town square. He walked through a narrow iron gate and into a courtyard where it was suddenly cool. Under his feet were large uneven stones. An impoverished place: mud houses, stones badly laid, carpenters who did not age their wood. Leo's grandmother had said about the American West: It will never be civilized. He came to an ancient screen door and knocked.

A woman inside rose from her desk and called to him to come in. She extended her hand. He shook it. "Why is the station so far from the town?" Leo asked, and she laughed. "Each one of you has a different question," she said, "but every one of you opens the conversation with a question."

The woman, Dorothy, gave him a short list of commands: Do not refer to yourself by your real name or call any of your colleagues "doctor" when on the streets of Santa Fe. You will be given a new driver's license without a name, and your address from now on will be Box 1616, Sandoval County, New Mexico. Your occupation will be "engineer." All of your mail will be read, both incoming and outgoing.

Dorothy arranged for a driver to take him to a dude ranch north of Santa Fe, just overnight.

"Who is that?" he asked the young woman driver as they passed a statue in front of the Catholic cathedral downtown. "That is Archbishop Lamy," she replied, and then she turned to him and smirked. "*Mr.* Lamy to you."

The next day the same girl picked him up at the ranch and drove him past a little collection of foothills studded with what he later learned were pinions, stubby trees with short needles. Between them was a fine loose gravel. It was very hot in the sun, cold in the shade. She came to a bridge over a wide, muddy river and then drove up a winding dirt road with frightening drop-offs to the top of a tableland. The ruts in the road were so deep, they looked to be made by elephants. Pinion trees lay beside the road with their roots pointing to the sky. When they got to the top, Leo saw strings of barbed wire and a tower with a man leaning against the side, and his heart froze in his chest. Mud, men building barracks out of planks, a large old lodge made out of what looked like the trunks of trees. Beyond the houses, mountains, a clear blue sky. "Nobody can think straight in a place like this," he said to the girl. "Everybody who comes here will go crazy."

Eleanor had been in New Mexico off and on for a little over three years. She and her cousin Betsy, an art dealer, took the first trip at the invitation of Mabel Dodge Lujan in Taos, who kept a kind of salon for eastern visitors—*everyone* had been to visit Mabel Dodge. After Eleanor arrived in Taos, she did nothing but sit on the *portal* of her guesthouse and look out at the mountains. She watched the aspen trees turn from green to gold from August to October. The clarity of light blinded her; shadows moved across the floor of the desert between the mesas like great flying dragons. An abundance of colors at sunset. She borrowed a horse called a flaxen mane and rode through aspens the color of deer, which grew so close together that she had to kick her feet out of her stirrups and hook her knees on either side of the saddle horn. In the dry, calm air she felt new to the world.

In New York, she had been attracted to some of its shapes: especially the new Chrysler building with its oblong windows and pointed helmet on top. Or the beautiful changing sky that she often rushed from the front door of the apartment to see. But it was not until she arrived in New Mexico that she found her landscape. It was as if the world had been thinned. The lush green Midwest and East had hidden what she craved: shape and bone and distance.

After she had settled in at the Lujan house, she mixed aureolin with water and watched it turn to pale gold-yellow like the tops of the cottonwood leaves. She tacked a piece of the paper to an old square of pine she found behind the kitchen and tried to make the paint match the leaves. It shimmered, dissolved; what she saw in her mind refused to release itself on the paper. She backed off, watched, then drew another leaf, mixed a trace of orange in with the yellow. It lay on the paper flat as a pancake warming in the oven.

She read in van Gogh's letters to his brother Theo: "I am trying to learn yellow. It refuses me."

After suffering Mabel's autocratic hostess style, and a little worried about Tony Lujan's affectionate glances, Eleanor traveled the next summer, not to Taos, but south, to Santa Fe. She stayed in a hotel a few blocks from the plaza and bought five tubes of color, two sable filberts, and a new canvas to celebrate.

The varnished cliffs at Arroyo Seco, a twisted cedar, the aspens in October, spoke to her. She wanted to create paintings of them that were clear and not frail or tentative, not pink portraits of women and children. To paint abstracts, paintings that did not tell a story but rather spoke of the wordless and silent, in a medium that was itself silent and without words. She wanted her work to say, I was here. I saw the world.

She had uncovered women artists as if discovering secrets: Marietta Tintoretto, sixteenth century (whose father, Jacopo, also a painter, dressed her in boys' clothing as a child so that she might accompany him wherever he went); Louise Moillon, seventeenth century, who made paintings of gleaming cherries and slices of cantaloupe and was mistaken for a Dutch male artist; eighteenth century, Marie-Denise Villers, in whose painting of a young woman drawing the girl is turning away from her window as if to shut out distraction; nineteenth century, Mary Cassatt. She had wondered if this was how it was, one per century? From their lives, she learned what it took to succeed—Louise and Mary, born into wealthy families or married into wealth—and what the odds were—Marietta, dead at thirty in childbirth.

She had done it once. She had painted pieces of her apartment in

New York: the large living room with a small table and a chair
stacked with books, a vase on the table with a green flower, a pale
violet wall and Edgar's overstuffed chair in the background in deep
blood red. She began with this domestic scene, to emphasize her sex
and her joy in her life with her new husband, and the painting gradually transformed into an abstraction. She used vertical lines and lavish layers of color. As she painted, she realized that it was not the
"chair" that mattered or the "table" but the space each created: their
shapes and then how the shapes reacted to each other. She felt as if
she were breaking up the structure of her living room, and seeing it
instead as color and light and shape. Her show at Edgar's gallery
sold out. A reviewer called her "an American (female) Matisse."
Walker Stern, an English collector living in Japan, had arrived late
on the opening afternoon and stood in the white rooms with the
paintings, and asked the price of two of them. They were Edgar's
favorites. He named an outrageous figure and Stern sat down across
from him and wrote out a check. It was more than anyone had ever
paid for a living painter's work. And yet some critics made jibes:
something "sensual" in this "woman's" work, the bed in one painting
was "very much in the foreground." A Freudian analyst was asked by
one magazine to view her paintings and give his opinion. Their
voices now combined with the ones already inside her head.

Then everything unraveled, and her own struggle began.

Her brother's letters reached her from the Pacific, where Teddy was
a junior-grade lieutenant on the Yangtze Patrol. He had met a man,
he wrote, who "could sight the curvature of the earth along a bar."
He had gone to a house where, the directions said, there was a coolie
at the gate with six fingers on his right hand. Once, growing sick of
the slack tide of a receiving line, he decided to introduce himself to
the ambassador's wife when he got to her as the "husband of some
cows in Indiana."

"Nothing happened," he wrote to Eleanor. "She smiled and said thank you."

After describing a forced march through rice paddies and dense green water, he wrote, "This is what in retrospect will be known as a lark." Then he was on a ship with a name he couldn't give her; pieces of the letters were blacked out or cut out so they felt like the paper crafts she and Teddy had made as children, snowflakes, stars, chains of paper dolls. She folded the letters and placed them in a sandalwood box, together with her grandmother's earrings, her baby pearls, and her beaded evening bag.

In those early months, Eleanor traveled the villages. In the dim churches, she found the Santos and Retablos. Our Lady of Sorrows holding a rosary, with a headdress made of flames. Our Lady of Guadalupe, Our Lady of the Rosary. Eleanor studied their faces, the various Our Ladies, in the tiny churches in northern New Mexico. In the Sanctuario at Chimayo, the lady was dressed in lace, like a grandee's wife, carrying the child, Jesus, as if he were her purse. Another baby Jesus wore silk garments and tiny baby shoes. Sometimes the baby's face was crowded next to Mary's cheek, his little neck bent upward and his eyes on her face. Mary's eyes were often on some distant, tragic point. Their skin was inevitably dark, a cloth over the head, hiding the hair. What did Mary's hair look like? Did she wear it in a braid?

At Chimayo, the crucifix was dark green with gold leaves painted on it. The body of Christ, Our Lord of Esquipulas, wore a long necklace of pine berries. In a dark inner room, a hole in the ground held healing mud, said to have dried up from a hot spring. On the wall, a handwritten sign read, "If you are a stranger, if you are weary from the struggles in life . . ." As Eleanor knelt at the edge and pulled red clay from the bottom and tied it in her handkerchief, the eyes of infant Jesuses watched her with plaster calm. Santa Coleta held a cross with an ear of corn behind her. San Acacio was dressed in a

Spanish suit with a long coat and decorative ribbons at the knees. With what looked like a theater curtain behind her, St. Mary Magdalene knelt in prayer.

At Penasco, higher in the mountains, she witnessed a procession for Palm Sunday. An elderly woman dressed in a round black hat and a polka-dot dress carried a pavilion for Our Lady with a man who looked like Teddy Roosevelt, with a walrus mustache and small round glasses. Beside them stood an Anglo woman with a long horse face, dressed in a white hat and white shoes and a dress that buttoned from the neck to the hem.

She thought at first she was seeking "things to paint," as Teddy used to say, or was a simple tourist in these churches, at those processions, but gradually she saw that she was a pilgrim. She wanted to go to a service, to sit in the pew, to repeat the words. She wanted to offer prayers for Teddy, not knowing what prayers really were, and for herself, not knowing even what she sought. At the Sanctuario, it seemed to her that prayers had gathered in the corners, like leaves.

One Sunday, she ate breakfast early in the hotel. Across from her two women traveling together looked out on the courtyard. A scrawny cat scratched himself near the smoke-smudged outdoor fireplace. One of the women said, as she salted her eggs, "In the evening, that courtyard has atmosphere. But at dawn's early light . . ." She gestured with her fork. Eleanor walked across the street to All Saints Episcopal Church. A few old people joined her at the early Eucharist; the families would come later to the eleven o'clock. "Almighty God unto whom all hearts are open, all desires known and from whom no secrets are hid," said the priest, a lean man with a neatly trimmed beard, about forty. When he placed the wafer in her hands, he smiled at her. She began attending the weekly Eucharist at seven-thirty on Wednesdays. It had none of the elegance of the calls described in the sermons of her youth; she felt pushed, prodded, tantalized. Saul falling into the ditch beside the road to Damascus, awaking blind.

Each time she repeated the same words, she heard a different voice. She came to desire repetition. All desires known. From whom no secrets are hid.

One morning, as she drank her coffee and read the *New Mexican*, she heard a footfall beside her table. Looking up, she saw the priest from across the street.

"May I join you?" he asked.

No, you may not, she thought, and said, "Yes."

"Bill Taylor," he said, and sat down. He wore his collar and a clean black shirt. His cuffs were turned back, his hands brown and callused, his nails filled with dirt. Noticing her looking at them, he said, "Gardening."

After he ordered coffee, he looked at her quietly. "I'm sorry to bother you," he said. She nodded. "I have of course noticed you coming to church, and I am not here to get you to join the altar guild." Eleanor smiled despite herself, and then, despite herself, she began to cry. Bill sat quietly, sipping his coffee. In a small voice, she said, "I feel as if a hand is pushing against my back."

"That's funny," Bill replied. "I felt as if someone were pulling me."

Eleanor looked up. The priest took the lid off the sugar and added a teaspoon to his cup. He looked over its rim at Eleanor.

"That's a relief," Eleanor said. "Would you like breakfast?"

"If you'll buy," he replied.

"I'll buy."

She liked to drive down the dirt roads near Socorro on the plains of St. Agustin where the roads were so straight, you could see them narrow to a point on the horizon. Sometimes, as she drove, she closed her eyes, held on to the steering wheel, and bounced on the seat, opened them again quickly, then closed them again for a longer stretch of time. At night, she turned off the headlights and drove by moonlight.

On the road to Dusty one Saturday morning, far ahead she saw a cloud that touched the ground. The sun was shining and she took off her father's wool sweater. When she reached the cloud, it was snowing inside. Snow iced the ruts. The Ford window fogged so that she could barely see the trees along the road. She put the sweater back on and pulled down her hat to cover her ears. Ahead, she saw a patch of blue sky. All at once, she was out of the cloud, the sun was high up in the sky, and the road was bare. Driving back, she dove into the cloud again. This time, hail shook out of it and beat the Ford's hood like ball bearings on a tin can.

As autumn neared, she knew she was stealing the days. In the late fall, she would have to return to New York, take the long train ride back, watch out the window as the desert receded and the plains began. All the way to Grand Central Station and the waiting car. She would be driven to the apartment with the wraparound terrace and the view of the East River. Stephen, the Irish doorman, would open the door and tip his hat. Upstairs, Edgar would be sitting next to the electric heater in that favorite tattered armchair, his octopus hands at the ready and the edge of his tongue prepared.

Sunday morning, September 8, 1943, she read an ad for ten acres of land west of town, near the Rio Grande. She drove out along Buckman Road, toward the river, past sagebrush and tumbleweeds. The Jemez Mountains stood up blue in the distance. Following the directions the owner had given her, she turned south past the city dump onto a barely discernible dirt track, two shallow depressions running parallel, bending the low gray grass. Off in the distance, near a fence, she could see a blue pickup. Lloyd Ballentine, he'd said. I drive a Dodge.

They walked together, she in her long skirt and desert boots and he in his overalls, limping from "rheumatoid." He'd owned the land for twenty years, he said, intending it for his son, but the boy had died at Pearl Harbor. He stopped for a minute, fingering a piece of cow hair on the barbed-wire fence. Eleanor stopped beside him, laid her hand on his arm. "My brother is in the Pacific," she said. He nodded. They walked the land for two hours. He showed her each boundary marker: to the southwest, a pinion tree shaped like a dwarf with a yellow strip of cloth tied to its top branches; to the southeast, a pole attached to a juniper. In the middle of the land was an arroyo that started in the midst of a meadow and ran west and south. "You might want to fill this in," Ballentine said. "Old retreads work good."

"I'd like to buy it from you, Mr. Ballentine," she said.

"Fine," he replied. "Will your husband be joining you?"

A shiver ran up her spine.

"Maybe so," she said. They agreed to meet at the bank on Monday.

"Could I stay awhile and walk around on it?" she asked.

He looked at her as if gauging her ability to cut pinion, then glanced at her roadster. "Surely, ma'am," he said, and limped on back to his truck.

After a few minutes she settled herself near the shallowest part of the arroyo, on the dry grass. She heard a croak like a frog's and looked down at her feet. The sun was warm, and she lay back with her arms behind her head and closed her eyes. Now that it was nearly hers, she let her love for it, which had been restrained in her chest, spill out like water from a pitcher of glass. She took some of the sandy soil into her hand, then rolled over and kissed the grass, laughing. Mine, she said to herself, the first thing that's only mine.

At the hotel when she got back, a boy stood beside the door to her room with a yellow telegram in his hand. When she saw him, she ducked into an open room and stood against the wall, her eyes taking in the destroyed bed, the dried egg yolk on the plates, the coffee cups with a lipsticked cigarette floating in one, as if her eyes worked on the world no matter what had happened inside it. Then she put her hands in the pockets of her skirt and walked outside. The boy handed her the paper and she went inside her room to get him a dime. Then she unfolded the paper and read: "Theodore Garrigue captured, Pacific. Believed to be alive. Will send news of where-abouts when we ascertain them. Henry L. Stimson, Secretary of War." Slowly, she sat down on the bed.

Leo woke up as the sun fell on his face from the window set above the bed. He rubbed his eyes, looked around the room: a chair painted bright red beside the bed, a cupboard of some kind with long doors across from it. A painting on the wall near it: an abstract of a figure seated in a chair, a woman wearing a black coat, with long blond hair streaked with vertical lines of color. A red armchair in the background. It was a bold, interesting work. Leo decided he liked it.

After his arrival in the fenced, guarded city, a young army private had shown him to the square apartment at the end of the hall. He put his suitcases on a narrow bed with khaki blankets folded at the foot, "U.S. Army" printed in block letters on the hems. He took some things out—khaki pants, two cotton shirts, waxed slicker, book of fairy tales, diary, slide rule, Lotte's drawing, his single remaining Cuban cigar. He left the rest of his things in his cases, locked.

He had sat down on the cot, lit the cigar. Then the knock at the door. Startled, he jumped to his feet. A tall fellow slouched in. He wore a porkpie hat and cowboy boots. He had blue eyes and was very thin. He told Leo who he was, and as Leo shook his hand, the stories the British told at the Cavendish lab crowded his head. The strange American who had had some sort of nervous collapse while working there, the feeling that he was a "bit of a gamble," the snubbing the English gave him. Oppenheimer handed Leo what he called "a primer"; it was twenty-four mimeographed pages, and Leo sat down on the little twin bed to read it. "The object of the project is to produce a practical military weapon in the form of a bomb in which the energy is released by a fast neutron chain reaction in one or more of the materials known to show nuclear fission." Leo put it down on the blanket. A crow made a noise outside like a rusty gate.

"It is just possible for the reaction to occur to an interesting extent before it is stopped by the spreading of the active material," Robert Serber had said on that first night in the library reading room where they had all gathered. Leo looked around. They looked so young, in their twenties. Serber was thin, handsome, owlish behind glasses. He had his back to them, writing on the board.

Men were working outside and on the floor above them, the noise of hammers and saws. During one of the later lectures, a workman's leg would burst right through the beaverboard ceiling. On that first night, Serber said, "The bomb . . . ," and Oppenheimer, standing in the back of the room, sent him a note to correct him: "The gadget."

"The critical mass for metallic U-235 tamped with a thick shell of ordinary uranium of 15 kilograms: 33 pounds," Serber wrote in his schoolboy scrawl on the blackboard. "For plutonium, similarly tamped, 5 kilograms: 11 pounds."

"Think of the heart of the gadget then like a cantaloupe of U-235 or an orange of Pu-239 surrounded by a watermelon of ordinary uranium tamper," Serber said.

He went on. He had a stutter. "The combined diameter of the two nested spheres would be eighteen inches. Shaped of such heavy metal," he said, turning away from the board and for the first time facing them, "it would weigh about a ton."

One of the young men raised a hand.

"Could something like that be carried in an airplane?"

"They are modifying a B-29 right now," Oppenheimer said.

Eleanor had waited for news of Teddy as if she were suspended over a pit. Each day she made herself leave the hotel when the mail arrived so as not to be waiting in the lobby. She lit tapers in the cathedral and in the Sanctuario at Chimayo beneath the brown Madonna who gazed past her head; she did not step on cracks. She held his old letters in her hands but did not read them. At night, she dreamed he was

walking away from her, sometimes in the hall of the house in Lake
Forest, sometimes at the camp in the Adirondacks, once on a street in
Chicago where as she reached for Teddy a man dressed in a dinner
jacket threw a bouquet of yellow roses at her and yelled, "Catch."
After a month, she woke in the night screaming. At breakfast that day,
she heard her name as she was reading the paper, looked up, and saw
a boy wearing a blue bandanna coming toward her with a letter.

> Dear El,
>
> Do you remember the Spanish chicken Cook used to
> make? It had onions and sliced white mushrooms. Garlic.
> Her face used to sweat, her rouge ran down her cheeks.
> Mother said it had too much seasoning. It must have
> been the jigger of cognac.
>
> Love, Teddy

They came one by one after that, every several weeks, recipes for
sauced poached sweetbreads, potted goose, Smithfield ham with
black pepper and cornmeal, lobster Americaine. She opened one and
the first lines read, "Allow 200 soft-shell clams, 5 broiling chickens,
4 dozen husks of corn." When she put it down she thought, He's
starving.

TWO

After Communion on Wednesday mornings, Bill Taylor liked to garden. Standing at the altar, his hands cupped over first the bread and then the wine, he thought sometimes of the caterpillars that curl into hollyhock leaves in late summer, weaving a gauze tunic with their mouths. That odd man David Stein, with whom Bill played chess, studied a little biology before he trained as a machinist at Brooklyn Polytechnic; he told Bill that after the cocoon is finished, the animal goes into a hibernation-like sleep, and then slides into what amounts to a genetic sludge. "He is reconstituted," David had said, gesturing with his cigarette over a cup of coffee at La Fonda, with his dry smile. "What is it you Christians say, 'He is risen'?"

Today, it was digging, mostly. The compost had to be dug into the dry sandy gravel that they call soil here. He had been composting all year and had discovered to his delight that red worms were now roosting among the rotting banana peels and old chili skins. He had a chili to plant, given to him by the Royce family after he had served as supply to the mission church in the little town of Hatch, a pretty little place near the Rio Grande in the south, famous for its red variety of chili. He had baptized the Royce grandchild that day, and they, dirt farmers, had presented him with what he knew was a home-grown prize. He had carried it back, nestled in a box like a jewel beside him, in the front seat of the old jalopy.

He had heard Eleanor's name before he actually met her. One of the sweet old women, Margaret, who had moved out from Connecticut for her TB, said "Eleanor Garrigue" behind him to Mrs. Stanley, who always made an appointment to talk of dark depravity and then had nothing to confess, and he turned to see the new woman with the dark hair who had cried during the prayer of reconciliation. As he shook Eleanor's hand, he felt in her a watchfulness born of one who has been hunted down. And a pitiful belief in hiddenness, like a gopher he'd seen in a field, starving in its hole as a hawk circled, hour after hour.

Later in the evening, as he sat on his bed, the last of the scotch in his hand, he had fished a memory out. The Garrigues of Lake Forest. Bill was then an associate in Rhode Island, one church out of the General Seminary in New York. He had left the brick buildings with their close of lawns and the peonies that bloomed white and pale pink in the spring, his sanctuary in Manhattan, for a dreary granite pile in Newport where the rain dripped onto the fair linen and the moody organist drank bourbon from a flask between services. Seeking a rectorship, he was asked to preside at St. Chrysostom's in Chicago, a church in the English Gothic style designed by the famous Chicago architect Rudolph Garrigue. The day before he preached, Garrigue and his wife had invited him for sherry at their modern house on the lake. Bill stepped into the entry hall, which had a brass directional set in the terrazzo floor. He was led through the dining room with an oval Biedermeier table and chairs of old-growth cherry slipcovered in heavy tawny silk. Sylvia Garrigue had purchased them in Paris. "She who commands," Rudolph had said, chuckling.

They sat together, sipping out of delicate crystal glasses, gazing out at the lake. Sylvia asked after Bill's family, and he replied that his father owned several department stores in Southern California.

"In trade?" she replied. "How interesting."

As he walked with Garrigue to the car that would take him back to the train for Chicago, they met the adolescent boy, the son—what was his name? A skinny kid with straw hair and a mischievous side-long smile. Adopted, Garrigue had said, once they were alone, and Bill was surprised. He looked like his father.

The boy had lived with his mother and her lover in an old shack next door to the Garrigue camp in the Adirondacks, somewhere on a lake, Garrigue said, and Bill could feel a confession coming. He had learned to sense it hovering in the air, a brief hesitation, then the spurt of words and the head turning away. He reached for the stole around his neck that wasn't there and grabbed his raincoat lapels instead. Rich, powerful men often confessed in a geographic inter-lude, he had learned—a walk to a car, standing at a men's room sink, during a smoke after dinner, when the barriers came down and then went up. No time for questions or further reflection. The mother's lover had been cruel to the child, only a toddler, Garrigue continued. He had beaten him, left him out in the cold. Bill could still see the late-afternoon Winnetka light, the fine white houses along the long lane, feel his own distraction at the hope of a new job, an escape from the Rhode Island pile, as he waited for the man to lift the burden off himself and give it to Bill (a rich man's version of confession), but nothing came of it. Sylvia wanted a second child, Rudolph had said as he handed Bill into the car, gave the driver instructions. And then, "So I hopped over the fence and came back with a baby."

The next day Bill had risen early and wandered Chicago until late afternoon. He loved that city, with its blustery lake weather, the green lions in front of the Art Institute, the beautiful paintings dis-covered by young women just out of finishing school on their first tours of Europe and bought by their doting fathers. Evensong was the high point of that high church's day. Chicago society was there to view Bill. He was all aglow in his pretty white alb and new cassock that his mother had ordered for him from London and from just a nip in the sacristy. He had a future ahead of him. Toward the end of the service, an old man picked his way down the aisle. He was dressed in what looked like a collection of filthy rags and was bent over so far, Bill thought his back might be permanently bowed. Bill watched his progress, as did the rest of the church. There was a wave of whispers, like a wind in wheat. The man settled himself in the frontmost pew. The deacon was watching Bill for a signal to eject him; Bill knew what he was supposed to do, but he made no sign. And when Bill said the blessing at the end of the service, the man stood up and made the sign of the cross back, simply, with a dirty hand. In that moment, Bill saw the kingdom spread before him, as if the beggar had opened a door. He was the first to bless Bill, and the last.

Sylvia Garrigue stepped up to Bill at the end of the service as he stood at the door. She wore black and white tweed, and a strand of baby pearls. She was a beautiful woman, with formidable cheekbones, dark brown, almost black hair, long tapering legs, and perfect posture. She removed her right glove and shook his hand with a firm grip. "Your homily was charming," she said. "The lectionary does provide us with rich readings, doesn't it? But I must ask you: do you always allow gentlemen who don't bathe to disrupt a service?" and he knew his chances of being hired were finished. She pointed out the glass windows above their heads, made in the "Connick studios in Boston," depicting Saint Elizabeth and John the Baptist and the war in heaven. One of them was given in memory of her friend Dorothea, she said, and she recited the text to him as if reciting a difficult Latin verse: "Let her own works praise her in the gates." They must have stood there for ten long minutes while she stretched out her rejection of him.

Now he was here, in this little place populated by Roman Catholics, Mrs. Stanley's need for confession, caterpillars, and the various mysteries. The mystery of Eleanor Garrigue. The mystery of David Stein, and his own inescapable impatience as he waited to know what help he could be to them.

He walked into his house to clean up. David was always punctual. After washing and changing into his clerics, he closed his front door, painted blue to keep out the *brujas*, the witches, and walked down Palace Avenue to the plaza. Pueblo women were sitting on old bedspreads in front of the Palace of the Governors under the *portal*. They were wrapped in old cotton blankets, blue and pink, nothing beautiful or handwoven. On sheets and bedspreads spread in front of them lay their wares: brown and white pots, necklaces of turquoise beads, a chain of animal fetishes and coral, a pot as black as pitch. Bill had never been able to stop and buy anything here; the poverty and beggarliness of the people filled him with despair and guilt. The air was cold, and clouds were gathering in the north. He had heard a story when he first arrived about a group of Indians from Taos who were gathering pinion nuts on a high mesa north of Santa Fe, near Truchas, on a sunny day in early spring. One of them felt the air change. Too late they started packing up. The storm dropped five feet of snow in two hours. Although a government plane dropped blankets, fifty of them died of exposure.

He crossed the street to take a look at the Civil War monument in the middle of the plaza, and saw Griefa Arnada coming out of the Capital Pharmacy. He sped up and managed to match his step to hers as she hurried toward La Fonda.

"*Buenos días,*" he said with his bad accent. "*Como estás?*"

"*Buenos días, el padre,*" she said. She was one of the few who were native here to call him a priest, and he was grateful for her courtesy. She added, picking up speed, "*Bueno y como la tamalera.*"

Bill laughed. "Me, too," he said. "I am also good and, like the tamale man, still selling tamales.

"How is Eleanor?" he asked, foolishly. "Have you seen her lately?"

"Señora Garrigue, I don't know," she replied. "*Adios,*" and she had abruptly turned right and escaped him.

He walked into the side entrance of La Fonda, past Lizette's overpriced dress shop and into the huge lobby, with its great dark beams and its deep leather chairs edged with brass studs. At a table in the courtyard, he saw David hunched, smoking, his big arms resting on the tiled table, reading the *New Mexican.* For a minute Bill just watched him. He was still, like a large bear, his shoulders stretching his shirt. He seemed perpetually a boy, a younger son, though Bill knew he was thirty. They had met maybe four times for coffee, always at David's invitation, after having been thrown together at Santa Fe's only chess club. When Bill had asked what brought him to Santa Fe, David had said his work was war-related, and that was that. Bill walked forward and sat down. David grunted a hello, still reading.

"Our boys have made it to northern Germany, I see," Bill said, reading the headlines upside down, the way he used to read his father's mail.

David looked up and nodded. "With the help of the Soviet army."

"Yep," said Bill, and ordered a coffee with cream, knowing it was not coffee but probably Nuveco, that ugly blend of soybeans, chicory, and a few genuine coffee beans. "It looks like they are near Magdeburg, a beautiful city," he added, doing what he called to himself his priestly prattle. "There is a church there with the most beautiful misericords, seats for monks to rest their haunches on while they pray, almost standing. They are carved underneath with figures of God knows what," Bill said, thanking the waitress. It was Lydia, who had a scar from a burn the size of a silver dollar on her left hand; she seemed to always wait on them. "Faces of little devils, a man beating his wife, a fawning woman with a rich man, all hidden under the seats. Sins under the haunch." He noticed David had returned to the paper.

"How is your wife?" Bill asked. David's wife, Naomi, had just moved from Brooklyn to Albuquerque, finally, after a year apart from her husband. David had said, with something of a grimace, that his brother-in-law was paying for the two-room apartment on Fourth Street.

David smiled. Bill was not sure how he felt about David, but he did like it that David, rare among men, openly loved his wife. "She has made the apartment just like a home."

David pulled out the chess set from the vacant chair, and the two began. "Your work?" Bill asked, having taken the two pawns into each fist behind his back, and placed them on the table in front of him for David to choose.

"Hours and hours," David said. "We work from dawn to after dark." He frowned. "Sometimes until after midnight."

That was more than David had ever said about his work, and Bill leaned forward, but just then Lydia appeared, poured some coffee into his cup, and asked if everything was all right, and after Bill replied that it was, David was deep into setting up the game.

Eleanor carried a tray covered in a blue napkin. On it was a bowl of broth, a hard-boiled egg in an enameled egg cup, and several small, rectangular pieces of toast, "soldiers," as Cook used to call them, on a white saucer, food her mother used to bring her when she lay feverish in bed. Leo sat up on his elbow, smiled. *"Buon giorno,"* he said.

"Buon giorno," Eleanor replied and thought, He's not Italian.

She placed the tray on the edge of the bed and handed him the spoon. He noticed that it was silver, that the cup of the spoon was thinned by use, that the handle was embroidered with a garland of roses. He dipped the spoon into the broth and brought it to his mouth; it was good, clear and warm; he felt it run into his stomach and almost cried with the easy tears of the recently ill. Eleanor saw his eyes brighten; she looked away.

"I'm afraid I can't remember my name," Leo said, shaking his head in what he hoped was a convincing show of confusion.

"Mine's Eleanor Garrigue," Eleanor said. "Did you swim across the river?"

"I suppose I did," replied Leo. "How do you do, Eleanor . . . did you say, Garrigue?"

"Yes. G-A-R—"

Leo held his hand up. "I know the name," he said, and then stopped himself.

"You do? That's unusual," Eleanor said, waiting for an explanation. Hearing none, she said, "Where did you come from? There is very little across the river here."

"I was camping, I think. Got lost," Leo said vaguely, remembering a line from a cowboy movie he had watched in the mess hall. "I must have hit my head."

"I can't quite place your accent," Eleanor said, looking out the window. "I believe you spoke in German when you were delirious."

Leo felt sweat in his palms. "What did I say?"

"I don't know, exactly. I don't speak German. It sounded like '*Rouse ous dem fo-ee-er!*' You said it several times, with great urgency."

"Did I?" Leo said. Then he sighed. "I am sorry. So tired."

He leaned back on the pillow and closed his eyes. He heard her cleaning up the tray, walking out the door. As she passed through the doorway, he opened his eyes and watched her feet in what must have been deerskin moccasins with single silver clasps. Garrigue, Leo thought to himself. An uncommon name. Charlotte Garrigue, the American, Tomáš Masaryk's wife, our "first lady." Now long since dead. It would not be possible that this woman was related to her? He ran his hand along the white plastered wall near the bed. What else did I say when unconscious? he thought. How long do I have?

Eleanor placed the dishes in the kitchen, gathered her things, marched out the door, and walked along the faint trail until she got to the arroyo. She climbed down into it and followed a path of deer tracks and rabbit scat along the flat, rocky bottom. She loved the arroyo, tucked just under the blue sky, protected and hidden in a sandy, banked world. The arroyo turned and widened into a meadow. She found a flat rock, set up her easel, and pulled watercolors from her pocket. One of the tall jackrabbits split out of the grass and bounded into the pinions. *"Donde menos se piensa,"* Griefa had said to her last winter, *"salta la liebre."* When you least expect it, a jackrabbit will jump out.

As she arranged the paints, two brushes, and a square of paper, she pondered the man in her house. She was to drive into town today for lunch with Father Bill, and then she had hoped to fetch a doctor, but she had remembered on getting up that Dr. Allina took Mondays off. Gas rationing was so stringent that she could not waste trips into town, and she did not have a telephone. She had planned it that way. It kept Edgar at arm's length. To eke out time to paint had taken nearly all her efforts, as if she were withstanding a siege. And nothing was going well. She painted and repainted but she couldn't find the note she had found before; she couldn't find the place she had once won.

But today she wished for a telephone. If she had one, she could consult Father Bill as to what to do with this man in her house, or simply call Dr. Allina up tomorrow when he kept office hours. But without a telephone, she was stuck, in the position of having to throw a sick man out of her house or waste time and gasoline to get help. Or drag him into town to St. Vincent's Hospital. She supposed she could do that. She had very little gasoline and even less time. In the fall, she would have to return to New York. The deal was struck: like Persephone, she spent six months in the air and the light in return for the dark months in Hades.

She asked herself why she wasn't more afraid of the man she had found. Her mother had raised her on stories of white slavers who kidnapped women off the streets of Chicago and sold them into bondage in some far-off Asian country where men liked their white skin. No more was said about what the men did with the women, but Eleanor's child's mind had known, by the tone of her mother's voice, that what the men did was at once violent and juicy, having to do with the thrilling, dangerous life of adults. She had not thought of them in years.

But this man could very well be some kind of robber or worse. He was, she was almost certain, lying about forgetting his name. She supposed it was possible; she had heard of amnesia victims. Hadn't she read about that unfortunate woman found wandering in . . . where was it? Terre Haute? In her nightgown. But when he had said he didn't remember his name, his blue eyes had left her face, just for an instant, and then returned.

Yet the truth was, she was not afraid of him. She had put him in her bed the afternoon she found him, and made up a bed on the wide railed couch in the living room for herself. Before turning in, she had placed a heavy bench on her side of the closed bedroom door. She knew that Rita would wake her in the night if he tried to get out. And Griefa's house was only a few miles away. Griefa herself would be coming over in a week to clean. But he was so ill, and helpless, she doubted he could even stand up for long. She had slept that night off and on, almost as well as she ever slept, with a complete stranger in the house.

What she had noticed that first night rather than fear was her loneliness. How the presence of this strange man made her feel lonely.

She ticked off what she knew about him, as if making a list. He was of medium height, and his arms and shoulders were, or had been until very recently, muscular. If he weren't so ill, he would have been quite nice-looking. He appeared to be cultivated: He spoke English in an accent that indicated another first language. And possibly German. Also, the word in English: *im-plosion*. What did it mean? In looks and accent, he reminded her very much of two Jewish men she'd met in Prague, on a trip with her father and Teddy, when she was just out of high school. They had gone to visit the Masaryk family, several years after the death of her father's aunt, Charlotte Garrigue, the wife of President Masaryk. They had stayed at the Hradceny Castle, which hung over the gold-tipped spires of the city. The president's son, Jan, had sent her and Teddy a note on heavy stationery enclosed in an envelope sealed with green wax. "Good morning! This being my 'receiving day in bed,' I'll be delighted to see all of you as often and as long as possible." It was signed, "Your old John."

She and her father had walked down a hidden staircase from the castle into the city, where he showed her the arched carriageway of the house belonging once to Kepler, and the red wheels and ostriches painted on the sides of buildings that served the Bohemians as their addresses until the Hapsburgs required them to use numbers. She had gone to a lecture on Kandinsky's *Point and Line to Plane* one afternoon at the university and met the two men, slightly older than she was, who took her out for coffee afterward at the Café Slavia, where the well-dressed widows of mill owners sat at tables next to elderly writers correcting manuscripts. Under the Slavia's globe lamps, the three of them had smoked and talked about Kandinsky and his ideas about the spiritual in art.

"He says the effects of colors," Eleanor had said, wishing to prove how bright she was, "are like vibrations of the soul. I like that. He says that yellow is disturbing and cheeky and white is not 'a dead silence' but one pregnant with possibilities." The men had listened attentively. As twilight approached, they spoke of Freud. One of them hoped to be an analyst. He had been to Vienna to see Freud's apartment, and had stood in the doctor's waiting room, "where Dora and the Wolf Man must have sat!" He had said that he wanted to free his patients from their families, to help them stop the repetitious "building of monuments to their losses." They had been courtly, ironic, and warm. It was their warmth that had stayed with her. As she sat in the arroyo, she wondered where those two men were now, and whether this man's accent could be Czech. That would seem almost impossible, and yet there was in his words something of that language's soft slush.

She scratched her ear and pulled a flask of water from her jacket pocket, poured it into a little metal cup. Using an old china saucer, she mixed burnt sienna and ultramarine.

She had thought of Teddy as she helped the man into her house. If he managed to escape from the prison camp, would someone help him? Would someone feed and care for him?

There were no prison camps around here—the parallel really didn't hold—and yet she felt that helping this stranger was like giving to a larger account, from which Teddy might draw if the time should come.

None of these thoughts helped settle who this man was. There were not too many professions to choose from in Santa Fe requiring multiple languages and a European air. Some kind of teacher? A wandering diplomat? Eleanor almost laughed. But that didn't explain his desire to avoid doctors. Then she remembered: he had called out the name of a woman over and over: Lottie. Or Lotty. I must tell him about that, she thought. If he really does have amnesia, the name of a person might help bring him back.

The day before she found him, she had begun an oil of one of the mesas, the black one to the west of her property, on the other side of the river. The mesa was said to be a sacred place for the local Indians. It was a beautiful shape, a flat, dark oblong that lay between yellow clay cliffs with dots of green cottonwood in them and the bright blue mountains that were still topped with a trace of snow.

She had begun the painting while seated in an arroyo on her little folding canvas chair, taking only one break at noon to drink water and stretch. In the late afternoon, an elderly Spanish woman had climbed down into the dry bed and walked over to her, gesturing with her hands until Eleanor finally understood she was asking what she was doing, a woman, alone, sitting all day in the sun in the middle of nowhere. Eleanor smiled at the memory. She had wiped down the canvas of the black mesa painting at the end of that day. It wasn't right. When she thought of it, she felt a rise of panic in her throat. It could be gone, her gift. She had managed it once, made paintings that were celebrated and sought after, and sold for more money than anyone had imagined. But now her hands were like sticks and her sense of color muted and dull. She could not make the shimmering things she saw in her mind. Instead, they moved down through her fingers and became changelings, monstrous shapes. She told herself to put her fear aside, to just keep going. Today, a little watercolor study, a few rocks in the arroyo. As she worked and was quiet, the small animal world asserted itself around her; a baby lizard crawled close to her foot, a horned toad sunned itself beside the easel leg.

She had loved watching her father draw at the desk her mother had bought for him, with the pewter lamps that were shaped like twin carp, their mouths open, black marbles for eyes. He usually wore the old brown sweater that she wore now.

She had asked Estaban to make a long window looking out at the mountains, under which she had set her father's desk. She often sat at it in the evenings, holding the old Lalique stamp tray in her palm.

Take heart in the smallest things, her father had said. Avoid the grand gesture. He taught her and Teddy poker, charades, murder; how to fish, fly a kite, and play softball. One night he called her over to his study window to look out on the lawn. In the last light, an ancient raccoon was sitting on her tail, her large belly spread before her, picking fleas off her stomach. "As if they are little shrimps at a cocktail party," her father said, laughing. Eleanor watched the raccoon's sly masked face, a study in endurance. In Prague, he pointed out a young woman in a starched white chef's apron on the street, her head thrown back to the sky as she hauled up the metal shades on a restaurant window.

Eleanor had sat on the floor beside his desk, drawing on her own little pad of paper as her father drew on his. When she was twelve, he took her on the train to visit New York and then Philadelphia. In that city, they went together to visit a friend of his, a woman who lived in a large, airy house with an iron gate. She was tall, almost as tall as Eleanor's father, and, although not pretty, had a direct gaze and an open face. Her house was filled with paintings. After tea one afternoon, the woman asked Eleanor if she would like to see something special. She then walked out of the room and returned with a shallow wood box.

"Open it," she said.

Eleanor pulled the lid sideways off the box, and found inside the stubs of used pastels, in every color. The pinks and roses were the most worn down.

"These belonged to Mary Cassatt," the woman said. "She was my aunt." Eleanor sucked in her breath. It was like touching a source. She traced her hands over the chalks, and her fingers came out tipped with dust.

When she was nearly graduated from high school, Rudolph helped her apply to the Art Institute in the city.

Eleanor stood up to survey the work, to let it show itself. She wished to be alone to paint—was that too much to ask? The animals scattered and she walked back toward the house.

THREE

L eo folded his hands behind his head. He could smell the faint pinion scent from the fire she had made earlier and see the coals glowing on the hearth. He liked having a fireplace in the bedroom.

He had gone to work in Los Alamos as if he were going to the Cavendish lab. He put on his pants and shirt and shoes in the morning, his slide rule in his coat, and walked outside into the dry air that smelled of bacon frying and pine needles. He walked past Bathtub Row and the house belonging to Niels Bohr, whom they forgot to call Nicholas Baker. (When the film *Madame Curie* was shown at the little theater in town, Leo had walked up to Enrico Fermi, alias Mr. Farmer, and asked, "How did you like *Madame Cooper*?") At the hutments, the boardwalks were strung with laundry lines; what's-his-name, the machinist, hung out his own boxer shorts, his wife being back in Brooklyn. He started to like American coffee again. He read Walt Whitman. He took a sleeping pill every night as he had ever since he and Fermi made the pile go critical in the squash court in Chicago and he saw the ghost of things to come.

He knew before he read the primer what it would say. As Serber wrote on the board, describing those innocent fruits—a sphere of plutonium, like an orange, a cantaloupe of uranium—he had looked sideways at Leo, and Leo had nodded his head. He was the one who had put them on this path.

On a gray day in September 1933, Leo Kavan was standing on a curb near Southampton Row where it passes Russell Square. He had been in London only a few months, having left Berlin one step ahead of the Nazis. Just as the light changed and he stepped forward, he wondered if there might be an element that, when split by neutrons, would emit not one neutron but two. He could not stop himself from following this thought even though he knew, even then, where it would lead. A release of energy on a grand scale.

Presidents and prime ministers leaned toward his lips after that moment; he made friends with Justice Felix Frankfurter, a Jew like him but one who had Roosevelt's ear. His name appeared on lists drawn up by men in foreign cities. James Conant, Arthur Compton, practical men. Before that, he was just a smart Jewish refugee from Czechoslovakia. Now he was the man with a key to power over the whole world.

Leo lay on the bed in the still adobe house. He realized that this was one of the first times he had slept without a pill. Working on the Project, as they called it, had been at first similar to the Cavendish. Smart men working together, debating the problems of fission, critical mass, the secrets of the nuclei. But, gradually, he began to see that there were differences. Cavendish was old school, fairly dotty. The labs were almost unbearably hot in August, and miserably cold in the winter. Lord Rutherford had that weird British allegiance to discomfort. The ancient skylights were streaked with filth, the plaster walls stained with blooms of damp. Everything was jerry-rigged. Leo remembered in particular the basement contraption that collapsed when overheated. Here, though surrounded by desert and mountains and the ubiquitous mud, the labs were spotless; some were air-conditioned. Someone told him it was the most expensive project in the history of the world. And of course there were the guards, the barbed wire that he never grew used to, the white badge

he had to wear to get into the Tech Area, and, finally, the great divid-
ing difference between the two labs that he saw only at the very end.

The pace on the Hill had been brutal. He had worked from early
in the morning to supper, gone back to his apartment, slept a little,
and then walked back. He had worked every weekend. There was no
time for reflection. Frisch, who was working on the problem of
implosion, was putting in seventeen-hour days. One evening last fall,
Frisch was running an assembly that had no beryllium bricks around
it, a "naked" assembly he lovingly called Lady Godiva. He leaned in
too close, and the hydrogen in his watery body bounced its neutrons
toward the bricks. Next to him sat Oscar, the family cat, who had followed Frisch to the lab as was his habit.

"At that moment," Frisch said later to Leo, "out of the corner of my
eye, I saw that the monitoring lamps had stopped flickering. They
were glowing continuously. The flicker had sped up so much that it
could no longer be perceived."

Frisch flung his hand across the assembly and knocked off some of
the bars. The lamps slowed down. The radiation he received in two
seconds was equal to a full day's allowance. For a human being, this
was survivable. (Two seconds more and the dose would have been
fatal.) Not so, as it turned out, for a cat. Oscar was taken to the army's
vet with an infected jaw, and the vet diagnosed radiation poisoning
and asked to keep the cat alive to see how such a new ailment pro-
gressed. Oscar's fur fell out in patches; his tongue swelled. Frisch
insisted, finally, that he be destroyed.

The men worked in the labs, and the wives lined up for rationed
milk and tried to cook on the woodstoves. The teenagers regularly
broke through the fence, just to outwit the army guards. "Wipe the
Jap off the Map" read a poster a teenage girl had over her bed. Social
classes were divided between scientists and nonscientists, although
Laura Fermi invited one of the daughters of a carpenter over to

dinner. It was the first time, Laura said, that the girl had eaten arti-
chokes.

There were parties every Saturday night at someone's room or one
of the larger houses on Bathtub Row. He did not know if the wives
knew what their husbands were doing in the lab. There was the
woman with twin daughters and a gold cocker spaniel named Toby
who arrived in a red convertible from Florida. She had brushed
against Leo, her scent filling the air. She asked him, later, in the middle of the night, as she lay beside him in his narrow bed, why he
smelled of gunpowder.

The women made elaborate American "snacks" for the parties:
pale cheese squares that someone had laid her hands on disappeared
in a matter of minutes. They drank a lot of gin. Oppenheimer made
impressive martinis. And punch made with 200-proof lab alcohol.
When Americans said, "I'm going to pack it in," it was a way of
announcing they were going to bed. Keep your eyes peeled, one of
them said. I'm going to spill the beans. They drank cowboy coffee,
ate peanut butter, and played five-card stud.

As he lay in the quiet bedroom, he remembered one particular
evening: all of them drunk. Oppenheimer's brother, Frank, with his
bug eyes and a chain-smoker's gravel-filled voice, singing *Take me
home, Irene.* Kitty Oppenheimer suggested a game of "murder" and
taught them all the rules. A deck of cards, one card for each of the
people in the room, the inclusion of the ace of spades and king of
hearts. Each person looked at his card. The person who had the ace
was the murderer. The person who had the king was the detective.
The detective was to go to a small, secluded place and wait. Then the
lights were turned out and everyone was to get down on his hands
and knees in the dark and crawl around. The murderer was to touch
someone on the shoulder and say, "You're dead." And then that person was to fall to the floor. If someone else happened on a body, he
was to find the detective and bring him to the scene. The detective

would turn on the lights, ask questions until he did or did not solve the crime. Only the murderer could lie. Leo had never heard of anything so ridiculous.

The cards were passed out. Leo looked at his. The nine of clubs. A victim. Laura Fermi announced she was the detective and withdrew to her bathroom, where she could be found, she said, in the empty bathtub. The lights went out. People were giggling, jostling, trying to move away from one another. A couple was kissing. Leo was surprised to feel suddenly frightened, taken back to the nursery, when the shapes in the dark were looming monsters, the room of his nurse too far away. Someone touched him on the shoulder. He flinched. "You're dead," said a man, a voice he recognized from somewhere. He fell to the floor, an old rhyme floating through his head. Kitty, giggling, crawled against his foot. "A body," she yelled. "Call the inspector."

Laura turned on the lights; Leo tried to sit up.

"You're dead," said Laura, pushing him back down.

She stood in the middle of the room, hands on her hips. He noticed other bodies, in shapes on the floor. The living sat around, some of them smoking. As Laura questioned Kitty, Leo from his floor vantage found himself watching a man across the room, the machinist. He was leaning against a wall, his black bushy eyebrows like caterpillars over his brown eyes, a cherubic face.

"Where were you when this body was found?" Laura had asked him, pointing to Leo.

"Across the room, over here," he had said, and laughed.

Stein, Leo thought. Penny-in-the-Slot Stein, one of the wives called him. You had to pay a penny to get him to talk. David Stein. He makes precision molds for the lenses. He had just lied. It had been his voice that told Leo he was dead.

What an odd thing to remember, Leo thought. But it was an odd place. There was very little theory, or, one would say, very little theory for theory's sake. In the air was the excitement of a gigantic undertaking, the most expensive project in the history of the world. And they were the smartest men in the world, isolated, surrounded by barbed wire and guards, and washed up on these shores by the war in Europe. Leo Kavan. Edward Teller. Niels Bohr. Bohr escaped from Denmark to Sweden in a fishing boat and then was flown to Scotland in a Mosquito bomber at 20,000 feet, above the reach of antiaircraft guns, but his head was too big for the helmet that contained earphones for communication with the cockpit. He did not hear the pilot's instruction to turn on the oxygen needed at that altitude, and he fainted over Norway.

Slotin, code named Stark, and Leo Kavan, Mr. Simms, worked with Frisch at Y-site, the highest security area, on the problem of finding the exact amount of critical mass, how much uranium was needed, the speed of collision. Slotin was in the habit of working the experiments without protective gear.

Slotin had become Leo's closest friend. He was very tall and shy, rural, precise, his hands large and adroit—in love with risk. He had studied biophysics at King's College in London, volunteered as a gunner in the Spanish Civil War. Leo was nearly his opposite: aloof, abrupt, urbane, a man who lived out of locked suitcases in hotels, had breakfast in drugstores, so absentminded he once boarded a train and then had to look at his ticket to remember where he was going, a physical coward. They argued politics.

"I have seen the dictatorship of the upper classes," Slotin had said. "I know it has its flaws, but I want to see the dictatorship of the proletariat."

"I don't want to see the dictatorship of anything," Leo had replied.

"That's naive," Slotin said gently.

"You were in Barcelona in 'thirty-seven," Leo said. "You called the waiters 'Thou.' "

"I was," Slotin said softly. "It was a state of affairs worth fighting for, although I did not always agree with it. And you saw how long it lasted."

On a rare day off, Slotin and Leo had visited the pueblo at the bottom of the winding road that led to the Hill, San Ildefonso, a collection of mud huts with straw sticking out of the plaster. Some of the technicians from the Project had wired the pueblo for electricity. The women from the place cleaned their apartments. The Los Alamos wives called them "half-days" for the hours they worked. One of the half-days had looked up at Leo once as he passed the schoolroom on his way to lunch, and he saw in her eyes a flash of wild sorrow that reminded him of his countrymen, a people so used to being invaded and occupied that they kept sane by aloofness and irony. Then the curtain dropped and she was a blank, fat, brown woman dressed in layers of calico. He wondered what it was like for her, to live within enemy territory, in separated land, what they called reservations.

Scrawny dogs wandered the broad dirt plaza, one of them with teats hanging down, a bad limp. Under a huge cottonwood tree, a woman wearing a long pleated cotton skirt sat in the shade, cooking stew in a blackened kettle over an open fire. A boy drew water from a well. Leo felt he had entered a primitive world, gone back in time. What he was doing on the Hill was as if in a future world, twinned with this one in geography but separated by time. The Pueblo Indians were living as if in the 1800s, perhaps farther back: their rituals carried down through generations. It was said that in a pueblo south of Santa Fe they still danced with snakes in their mouths. Leo knew of nothing in Europe to compare with it, one's primitive past living next door, like a living memory, or an admonishment. A man with a braid down his back leaned against the wall, a torn blanket thrown over his shoulder. Another man lay on the dirt, fumbling for his zipper. Dust, tumbleweeds. Slotin said miserably that they had seen a colonized people.

Slotin and Leo had one goal in mind: to defeat the Germans. A kilo of uranium might be equal in destruction to 20,000 tons of TNT. Would it be identical or greater than the explosion in Halifax Harbor, that accident in 1917 by which human destruction was measured, when the ship *Mont Blanc,* carrying a cocktail of dynamite, gun cotton, and picric acid, blew up and killed 2,000 people in one winter afternoon.

"A little bomb like that," Slotin had said one afternoon as they took a break, holding his hands in the shape of a ball, "could make it all disappear."

Leo had received the letter from Prague dated October 19, 1941, two months after it was sent. The memory of that letter was like lifting the first card of those toys made of cards stitched together with ribbon that then unfold all at once. The woman who wrote to him was the librarian at Charles University. She had seen Lotte at the train station among the luggage and the food, his Lotte, among the ill and the dying, crying babies, and a short, thin man who sat on his suitcase practicing a Beethoven concerto on his violin as if nothing were going on around him. Lotte was wearing a gray dress, the librarian said, a blue ski parka under her arm, and she was talking to a man in a black suit who sat with his hands folded on the handle of a furled umbrella. "She looked very brave," the librarian wrote, "but very pale."

Which foreheads were marked with a smudge of blood? Leo received the letter in Cambridge, on a brisk, cold day. He had been walking, again, to solve the problem of controlling the reaction. While he was out, the letter slid into his box behind the hotel's desk like a crisp, cold knife. When he read it, Lotte had been in the camp for two months. He read the letter, and turned, and he saw her, carried downstream, while he had been eating or opening a window or, God forbid, laughing. For some months afterward, he could not think, could no longer theorize. He worked on small technical problems. He hoped for any gain, any stride.

He left the Cavendish for the United States, to seek its assets. He worked in Chicago in the soot and the grime. The year he received the letter from Oppenheimer, inviting him to Los Alamos, the British bombed Hamburg in the summer heat until, an hour into the bombing, the streetcar glass and the roadways melted and the women and the children were stuck screaming in the asphalt on their hands and knees. He greeted this news with pleasure.

He worked his fingers to the bone. He loved the fierce determination of this young country, and its democratic idealism. Most of all, he loved its millions spent on the Project, and its young men, dying by the thousands, to save his sister's life.

Leo shifted in the bed and looked out the window. It perfectly framed a distant tableland, a dark oblong set in the landscape like one of his grandmother's obsidian brooches. He pondered just exactly where Los Alamos was from here. He had been barely conscious for most of the drive from the river to this house. He wondered just how well hidden he was. In some ways, he could not have made a better plan than this accidental one. Write a note to Frisch, disappear into the mountains through the teenagers' hole in the fence, and then fall into someone's house, as down a rabbit hole, a place owned by a woman who lived alone out in the middle of nowhere, who had no idea what lay just beyond her sight, almost certainly on the other side of that black mesa.

Leo heard the screen door swing shut as Eleanor walked into the house, and he settled himself against the wall, hoping to display a convincing patient-like weakness. In truth, he was feeling stronger. This odd limbo in this strange woman's house would be over soon. He had to get on with his plan, such as it was. He watched the door and wondered what she would be wearing today.

Eleanor picked up her library books, her purse, and her grocery list; Rita wagged at the door.

She walked into the bedroom and said to Leo, "I'm going into town, and—"

"Say hello to everyone for me," he said, and smiled. She was wearing a white shirt and a dark red skirt with a belt of silver decorations the size of dimes. Her hands were beginning to tan.

"I'll be strong enough soon," he said. "Please don't speak to anyone about me."

His tone was firm; the sentence was almost an order. Eleanor felt slightly off balance. Was he a man used to giving orders?

"You must see a doctor," she replied. "I will ask my minister to bring a doctor out here tomorrow."

Leo was silent. He tried to calculate the odds, how much to tell her that would keep her quiet versus too much that would send her running to her . . . what did she say? Her minister?

"Who are you?" she said into his silence. "Do you really not know who you are?" Then she remembered. "You said a name, when you were talking in your sleep. You said the name Lottie."

Leo grimaced and looked down at his hands. He had apparently told this woman everything about his life while out of his mind.

"My sister," he said finally, looking up at Eleanor. "My sister, Lotte, who is imprisoned in Lodz, a town, now a ghetto for Jews, in Poland."

Eleanor sat down in the little painted chair by the bed.

"I am grateful that you found me," Leo said, clearing his throat. "I did not hit my head." He stopped. Then said, "It is next to impossible to tell you more."

"I think you'll have to," Eleanor said. "I don't like being spoken to in puzzles."

Women, Leo thought. They take everything personally. And this particular woman was remarkably headstrong.

"Listen," he said. "I will leave soon. In days. And there is nothing, in any case, that a doctor can do."

She stared at him.

"What do you mean, there is nothing a doctor can do?"

"Nothing."

"So you are a doctor, too, as well as being Italian?"

A pause.

"I am, as you know, not Italian," he said. "And neither am I a doctor. But, you can believe me, I know what is wrong. It is, how shall I call it, a new ailment, as new to the world as its cause." He glanced at her and thought, You will forgive me, stubborn woman, for making a medical guess, but I don't think there is a cure.

Eleanor observed him, tilting her head. He was watching her carefully. She could hear the ticking of her watch.

"This is hard to sort out," she said. "But I am very sorry about your sister. My brother—he is in the navy—is in a prison camp. He is in Japan somewhere. The Japanese . . . they are starving them. I am so afraid that he won't be able . . . He was always thin."

Then she looked at her watch. "Oh, dear," she said, getting up. "I am late. I have to go."

Where exactly is this camp? Leo thought. What part of Japan? If he should succeed in his perilous task, would this woman's brother, and the many other prisoners, survive? And if he did not succeed? Did the American military know where the prisoner-of-war camps were?

Finally, he said, "You and I have something in common. Those we love are beyond our reach."

"Yes," Eleanor said, and smiled at him. "That's a lovely way to put it." Then she turned toward the door.

"Before you go," he said, "who made the painting on that wall?"

"I did," she replied, looking over her shoulder at him.

"You did!" Leo said.

"I did," Eleanor repeated, lifting a brow.

"I do apologize," Leo said, and then he smiled. "I seem to be a most awkward guest. It is quite extraordinary."

Eleanor laughed, and then fumbled for the key to the Ford in her purse.

"I am late. I have to go," she said.

"Goodbye," Leo said.

Eleanor rushed out of the house, nearly slamming the door on Rita, who slipped through and looked up at her with reproach. She got into the Ford, pulled her skirt in after her, and reached across to let Rita in on the other side. She started the engine, noting the gas gauge that never seemed to register properly. As she drove too fast into town, she thought over the conversation. An intriguing man with a secret and a sister, Lottie, in a Polish ghetto or camp. This would mean he was Jewish. She considered briefly her mother's view of her keeping not only a strange man, but a Jewish man in her house. And what had he said about what was ailing him? "As new to the world as" . . . what was it? And the last sweet phrase, "beyond our reach." That was it, perfectly. It was not until she was driving up Palace Avenue to park her Ford that she realized she still didn't know his name. He had managed not to tell her.

Bill waited at the Shed. Most of his time as a priest was spent waiting. No one had told him this in seminary. He surveyed the room from his little table near the front windows. One of the walls was painted green and had a painting of a large hollyhock on it, in pink. The doorway was so low, he had had to bend down to get inside. Under its arch, someone had hospitably nailed a bit of padded cloth. The Shed was a warren of rooms like this one, with strange colors on the walls and little tables packed with Anglos having lunch. Bill had never figured out how many rooms there were. The floor under his feet was uneven; he noticed that one of the boards was repaired with a bit of metal, like a hasp. At the end of the room in which he was sitting a purple curtain hung over a niche in the wall. He had glanced at the menu but knew what he would order: red chili blue corn enchiladas, flat, not rolled, which would come bubbling hot on a blue pottery plate, and a glass of iced tea. For dessert, chocolate cake. He salivated and smiled. Jim Sargent from the Santa Fe Country Store, that little place that sells oxford cloth shirts for the men and tweed skirts for the women, had lit upon Bill and his collar and taken him to the Shed after he'd been in town only a few days. Bill could never quite decide what drew him to the Santa Fe Country Store, with its bow ties and dress socks, and its light smell of bay rum: was it a harmless eastern fantasy, a haven from bolo ties and cowboy boots? Or a subtle elitism?

"You'll never recover from the Shed," Jim had said, settling his napkin into his lap. "You will dream about it when in foreign places."

Bill did yearn for blue corn enchiladas bubbling with cheese flat on a plate at least once a week. He had grown accustomed to sopapillas, little pillows of light dough; he'd bite off a corner and pour honey in without a second's thought. New Mexico, which had seemed so foreign to him when he had arrived, was now part of him. He could not imagine living anywhere else.

As he waited, he prepared himself, as he had taught himself more or less to do in his first years of priesthood. What is God's prayer for Eleanor in me? he asked himself. As if I knew, he thought. A young woman. Midthirties? Thoughtful, independent, brave, really, he said to himself. Very brave to come out here and live alone, and paint. She was careful with her money, but she had enough. Maybe just enough.

Every person was a mystery, he knew now, having been a priest for ten years. Almost every person had a secret. The secret was often tied up with each person's destiny, not to be confused with a preordained destination. No, it was more complex than that. It was as if each of us had another, deeper life than the one being lived. It lies underneath our ordinary days, our errands, the doing of dishes, the writing of letters, the making of money, like something moving, lobsterlike, under water. This only partially understood life (refused, often; banished, easily ignored) might be what we call the soul. The desire to know about it causes us to pray. But all the while, it's moving *toward* something, as surely as we are advancing in our lives, through careers, marriage, children. Every now and then, this hidden life surfaces, as if to enact itself, to bring something to fulfillment. Often, this happens when it intersects with another's. Bill had seen it happen; it was like a glimpse of things in that peculiar, vivid light after a rain.

He saw Eleanor coming through the courtyard. Her hair was a little messy, and her shirt could have used an iron. But she's stylish, he thought to himself. Her own style. He liked her enormously, he fully realized today, watching her stalk across the courtyard like a brave soldier. And she was running from something, that much was clear.

He stood up when she reached his room, after having, he knew, wandered around the restaurant.

Eleanor smiled when she saw him. He saw her face relax. Bill wondered, not for the first time, how she might feel about him.

"I am sorry I am late," she said. She looked at her watch. "But I believe I am under the ten-minute limit."

"By my watch, you are slightly over," Bill said.

"Let me see," she said, and pulled his wrist toward her. Bill was surprised by the heat of her fingers. She had flecks of paint on her left hand. She looked up at him and grinned. "No, I believe you are mistaken," she said, pointing to the watch's face. "You see now it is eleven minutes, but when I came through the door—"

"Ah, but I believe our deal is when you sit down."

"I am not sure we have agreed to that."

"Such a niggler," Bill said. "Okay, today we split the lunch. But next time, next time, you will buy. I know it."

"Don't count on it," Eleanor said, and picked up the menu.

"Is tomato juice still rationed?" Eleanor asked.

"Yes," Bill said. "No Bloody Marys, not yet."

Eleanor laughed. "Gin at noon. That's my brother's purview."

"I myself look forward to the return of gin and tomato juice at noon," Bill said.

Eleanor toyed with her spoon. She was about to tell him about the stranger in her house when she remembered the look in the man's eyes as he told her about his sister. Wait, she told herself. Wait a little longer.

"Have you heard anything more?" Bill asked.

"Not for three weeks," she said quietly. Then, "I have come to hate them, the Japanese. In occupied China, the paper said, they injected civilians with poison."

Bill nodded.

"Is it wrong, finally, to hate them?" she asked.

"No," Bill said quickly. "No, I would not say wrong. I would say understandable." He thought of the man who tended his mother's garden in Pasadena. His small fingers managing his beautiful tools, the rose cutters with handles shaped like round eyes. His gentleness, his soft voice, and the way he taught Bill to trim roses when he was twelve, when the adults were drinking on the terrace and playing bridge. He was somewhere in Arizona, all of his tools hidden in the garden shed, shoved into Bill's hands at the last minute before he was marched away.

"But not, finally, good for you. I mean, that's the problem with hatred. It's like taking poison and waiting for the object of your hatred to die."

"When Hitler surrenders, will they send more men to the Pacific?"

"I suppose so," Bill said. "I hadn't thought of that."

Their food arrived, and Bill wondered what he could say that might comfort her.

"Eleanor," he said finally, "is it that you are surprised by the persistence of evil?"

"Yes, Father Bill," she said, looking up. "I am."

"Just Bill, please. Me, too," Bill replied.

Then he added, "I know how much your brother means to you. You told me once that when he worked with a surveyor—was it in college? He said in order to survey, you must have two points."

She was looking straight at him, her fork in her hand.

"He is like your other point," Bill said.

She placed the fork on her plate and pushed back her tears with the heel of her hand.

"I seem to be always crying when I am with you," she said.

"Professional liability," Bill replied.

"Teddy was always the one I went to, to sort things out, in the family, to get a point of view," she said. "We'd compare notes on Father and Mother. Parents are such huge things otherwise—not even people, more like forces of nature. I've always felt sorry for only children."

Bill, an only child, replied, "I have met your parents, as you know."

"Yes, I know. You told me. That's such a funny coincidence. I don't think you've told me what you thought of them."

"Formidable," he said, laughing. "Charming." He stopped. He had not told her of their part in his loss of the job. Then he continued, "Does Teddy know he was adopted?"

"Father told him when he was ten. He told us both. I was twelve. He told Teddy in his room and me in mine. We'd always celebrated Teddy's birthday on Christmas Eve, and Father told us Teddy was our Christmas present. Teddy really took it in stride. He told me later he had guessed. I was astonished. I remember thinking that the world was way off kilter. I hadn't known this very important thing, my own brother. I started crying and couldn't stop. I told Father I was crying because poor Teddy was adopted, but I wasn't really crying for Teddy, but for me. I felt as if things were not as they seemed, if you know what I mean. A secret had been kept from me. I couldn't trust my own senses."

Eleanor took up her fork and finished her enchilada. Bill took a sip of tea. She was done, he could see, and he searched for a quick change of subject.

"How is the painting . . . ?"

Eleanor looked stricken and Bill felt immediately sorry.

"Forget I asked," he said. "Let's talk about something else. How about dessert?"

"Excellent idea," Eleanor said. "I'm sorry."

"I wish you well, Eleanor. I hope you know."

"I know you do, Father Bill. I mean, Bill. Thank you."

"I feel we must have the chocolate cake."

"Yes, we must."

FOUR

David Stein walked past Dr. Kistiakowsky's little stone house that had once housed the power generator for the school, renovated by Oppenheimer just for Dr. K. The army had painted "T-55" on it in chalky paint. David liked to get up early and walk to work, even though S-site was as far away as possible from the rest of the Project's buildings. The air was clean and cold. He passed the Ready-Cut houses, the army Jeeps outside the makeshift hospital, and Technical Building X, a board-and-batten-frame building painted in army green that housed the cyclotron. Mud was everywhere. Garbage cans overflowed. It reminded David of some neighborhoods on the Lower East Side in Manhattan, a vast tenement desert under perpetual construction. He stepped over a child's toy truck embedded in mud. He walked along the road to the site, and made his way around the twenty-five-foot earth and log barrier just outside its entrance. Oppenheimer had it built—"just in case."

David's formal job at Los Alamos—the job on the books, as his boss put it—was to machine the lenses that, when fitted together, would focus shock waves inward, toward the plutonium core of the gadget. They built molds, and filled them with high explosive, which they then "cooked" and pushed out of the molds like cakes from tins. The lenses had to focus shock waves uniformly, evenly, like waves on a beach. Hundreds of them must fit together to a precision of a thousandth of an inch. For each of the experiments, more molds. David kept a record in his logbook. By late March 1945, it had reached 20,000.

David's immediate supervisor was Dr. Kistiakowsky, and he liked him even though Kistiakowsky, an excellent horseman, had served in the White Russian Army. Kistiakowsky didn't believe in the American army's desire for secrecy and compartmentalization. "There is no way of knowing beforehand," he had grumbled to David, "which man is likely to discover and invent a new method that will make the old ones obsolete."

Kistiakowsky had studied John von Neumann's theory of how to win at poker, and he wished to prove it. Late at night, before going to bed, Kistiakowsky liked to play with a few men, Ulam, and the little machinist, Ernie, who could lift a lens weighing more than he did, and, sometimes, David. They played five-card stud, and then a game Kistiakowsky had invented called "Hillzapoppin."

David and Kistiakowsky had spent most of the early spring up in those hills, stuffing polonium and barium into the "screwballs," as Kistiakowsky called them. They inserted the initiators and plugged the holes with bolts, then waited to see what the implosion told them.

Polonium was a most expensive item, requiring painstaking care: Goldschmidt extracted it from old radon capsules from a cancer hospital in New York and sent it to Thomas in Dayton, who purified it in the makeshift laboratory he had constructed in his mother-in-law's indoor tennis court. Thomas then sent it to Los Alamos on platinum foil in a sealed container but, as was its habit, it translocated on the trip west, like a ghost moving through a door. David and Kistiakowsky found the polonium embedded in the sides of the shipping container. All this work and expense, David thought, to build a weapon, this "gadget," when children in Harlem were eating cornstarch to keep from starving. I am a free man, he said to himself that morning; I have established my very being outside the restraints of society. Thomas, that capitalist, with his rich mother-in-law and her tennis court. What these men have and what they do with it. Behind every great fortune, a great crime. But he felt bad about lying to Kistiakowsky.

As David arrived at the site, he remembered his first morning here. He had hitched a ride with a WAC who flirted with him as they bucked over the potholed road. When they got to the site, the first thing he saw was a huge man sawing a piece of high explosive on a box. The man had his knee pressed against it as if it were a block of wood. His left hand held a hose and directed a stream of water onto the saw in his right hand. He had nodded to David.

"No need for a safety marshal here," he said, and shrugged.

Kistiakowsky's men were the elite, who kicked around high explosive as if it were children's wood blocks. The men knew why S-site was so far away from the rest of the Hill. But the roads over to the site had been particularly bad, with ruts you could lose a child in. Kistiakowsky didn't like transporting high explosive over craters. He couldn't seem to get any action about fixing them, though, until earlier in the year when Leslie Groves, the army general in charge of the Project, visited for a few days. Kistiakowsky put wooden blocks under a Jeep's springs to make them inoperative and then insisted on driving Groves to the site. The road was quickly improved.

The safety marshals never lasted. When Kistiakowsky's men hit the molds, the safety men ducked and paled. One day, a man taking ground barium nitrate from the micropulverizer into an aluminum can had been knocked flat by the static charge. He got up, dusted himself off, and laughed at the marshal, who had fled outside. There was nothing else to do. You had to pretend you were deathless. A man named Joe supervised the men who coated the molds to keep the high explosive (everyone called it the HE) from chipping with the same varnish used to finish a bar. He made up a rhyme:

The varnish at S-site is bar top
To keep the HE tip-top.
If it doesn't work out,
At least we can shout,
And use the HE for a beer shop.

David walked inside to begin melting down the high explosive. Compound B was the fast-burning component and Baratol, the slower one: a cocktail of barium nitrate, aluminum powder, and a dash of TNT. He put the blocks in jacketed stainless-steel candy kettles. When one was melted down, he poured the liquid from the kettle into a rubber bucket and from the bucket into the steel hexagons and pentagons that were the molds. Small tubes were fastened on the inside of the steel to circulate water. He watched it, as Kistiakowsky said, as if it were an egg hatching, hoping to prevent air pockets from forming as it cooled by changing the temperature of the circulating water. X-rays had exposed air bubbles in the interiors of the molds; there were chipped corners and cracks.

Last night, Kistiakowsky said, he considered fixing the cracks in the molds with kitchen grease.

David had scored high on mechanical aptitude tests. The scientists might have prizes and theories, their parties and their bathtubs, but without his expertise, they could not succeed. His wife had to live separately from him because he had no status and there was no more room on the Hill; she was 100 miles and often three or more hours away by bus. His beloved Naomi, who had pale skin, hair like a flock of goats, and a mouth like a thread of scarlet. He worried about her, alone in the apartment in Albuquerque's flat and uneventful downtown. She might lose her ripeness. The others' wives were right here, fixing snacks and gossiping over the laundry. He had made a map of Los Alamos, a list of the leading scientists on the Project (it didn't take him very long to learn the real names—hardly anyone stuck to the fake ones). He had given the collection to Naomi, who sent it to her brother. He had figured out a great part of it from snatches of conversation picked up here in the special engineering detachment. The scientists rebelled against the army, like students in a private school run by a headmaster not as bright as themselves. This helped David do his work. Just last week, one of them told him how close they were getting to the exact amount of plutonium needed to make a bomb, as if they were chatting about a chess problem over their lunch of peanut butter and jelly sandwiches.

He worked slowly, methodically: measuring the wax, pouring another mixture, cooling it in the refrigerator, checking the molds made last week for more cracks.

They made molds from cardboard stuck together with Scotch tape. The HE was removed from the molds by various methods, among them hitting it hard with a mallet covered in rawhide and a bronze screwdriver. The assemblies were fitted together on wrestling mats.

Kistiakowsky walked in, greeted David, and made his way over to a kettle. Scrap was already collecting nearby. A man who had never spoken to David, a fat man who seemed always to be short of breath, was breaking up the big pieces into smaller ones for the burn by hitting them with a heavy rubber mallet. Just as David turned to him, a piece flew up from under the mallet and straight into his mouth. Before he could stop himself, he swallowed. His eyes bugged out. Kistiakowsky swore and ran over to him, slapped him on the back, but it didn't come back up. David only stared.

"Take a break, John," Kistiakowsky said, and the man, rubbing his throat, walked dazedly outside.

"Now we start a new experiment among many, Davey," Kistiakowsky said ruefully. "Whether high explosive can be digested, and, if so, does it remain flammable?"

Every day, the scrap was collected and burned in an area at the east end of the building. For the burn it was spread out in a single layer. Pete, a man who stuttered, was in charge. While they were all cavalier about the assemblies, they were respectful of the burn.

David hunched over the molds, varying the water temperatures, almost singing to them. He saw Kistiakowsky outside, pacing with his hands in his pockets, kicking at a tumbleweed that rolled across the boardwalk. When Kistiakowsky walked back inside, David turned and risked it.

"Do we know, yet, when we will test the gadget?"

Kistiakowsky looked at him sharply, his eyes black and dark.

"Just do the work, Davey. It has to get done."

David turned, hurt and resentful. Secrets are only for the elite, he thought. I let myself believe we were friends, but we are not. There can be no friendships between classes. He doesn't trust me because I am a mere machinist. He will be surprised when he discovers who I am.

As the day wore on, the burn scraps were beginning to mount up. The men raked the chunks into a shallow layer, like spreading out thatch. It was always tense before the burn. Some men found an excuse to leave the area. David had done this himself, and then felt ashamed. Now he always stayed, but inside, away from the windows. Pete whistled as he walked outside. Silence. And then a deafening explosion. Before he could think about it, David threw himself on the ground and rolled under a lab table. All around him men were swearing and running. Smoke and explosive hung in the air. David's hand was shaking. He saw Kistiakowsky get up and head toward the burn.

Pete came in, and tried to speak. His stutter was like a saw. Kistiakowsky put a hand on his shoulder. "The b-b-burning," Pete said. It's going to take him three minutes to say it, David thought, and he got up and walked outside.

FIVE

Eleanor rose on Sunday morning. The cold floor bit into her toes as she walked down the short hall to the bedroom where Leo was sleeping. She tiptoed in and reached into her *trastero* for the dark navy. She pulled the dress from the cabinet, ran her fingers through her hair, and walked out of the room to put on the coffeepot.

Leo watched her through nearly closed eyelids. She was going somewhere, wearing a dress. Where was she going?

In a short time, she came back into the room.

"Good morning," he said.

"Good morning," she said, then, "I am off to church."

He looked at her face. She had high cheekbones, and in the dress, she looked suddenly beautiful.

"You look *chic*," Leo said.

"*Gracias,* as we say here," Eleanor said, and smiled. "You look better."

"I'm feeling better."

"I'm glad," she said.

"You have been a very good nurse. I'll be on my way soon. And we can remember this as a strange interlude in both our lives." He smiled.

Eleanor felt, unaccountably, sad.

"Yes," she said. "We will. Sometime, perhaps, I will even know your name."

"Oh, yes," Leo said. "You will."

. . .

The air outside was cool and clear. As Eleanor drove to church, she realized that it was Easter Sunday and April Fool's Day all in one. She thought of St. Paul and how he said he was a fool for Christ. Maybe I'm a fool, too, she thought. Maybe it was foolish to have kept this man in my house. But he would be on his way soon, and they would remember this as a "strange interlude." How would he depart? Simply walk away? Or would he want her to take him into town?

She passed the little store on the way into town and waved at the man sitting on the porch. She switched gears as she came to a bend in the sandy road. A roadrunner skimmed across the road in front of her and she braked, and the Ford fell out from under her. She held the wheel tight, trying to remember what her father used to tell her about how to steer in a skid, and the Ford floated on the road until it finally stopped against a low bank on the right side. Eleanor got out and leaned her back against the hood. Her hands were shaking.

I miss him, she thought. I still miss him. Two weeks after her father had died, she dreamed a neighbor woman walked by and talked to her through the kitchen window. "I am moving," the dream neighbor said. "I am taking the dogs." And as she spoke, Eleanor's ghost father walked behind her, and, turning to Eleanor, tipped his hat, his hair sticking out like feathers. The dead appear so alive in our dreams; we carry them inside us. Eleanor dreamed her father had moved to Atlanta, Georgia, a place she had never been. It was, she realized on waking, a way to satisfy the question that is asked over and over when someone dies: Where is he? Where did he go? In Atlanta, her father was living in a house with bar stools and with lace doilies on the furniture. "Your mother doesn't want to move here," he said.

When Eleanor rushed into the hospital room directly from the train station in the middle of the night, Rudolph opened his eyes and said, "Oh, it's you. Don't leave me alone."

She and her mother had taken turns sitting with him. He died a few minutes before midnight the following day. Eleanor told Sylvia she would leave her there with him, and she walked out into the hallway. A nurse brought her tea. Sylvia came out a few minutes later, and the nurse found her a chair. Eleanor walked in and sat down next to her father's bed. She held his old, rough hand and sobbed.

Finally, in the early hours of the morning, she took her mother home, in a cab, to the big house, dreading the empty, hollow rooms. Instead, when they walked in, she felt that the house had been warmed as if by fires of welcome. She sat with Sylvia on the couch in the living room and held her hand. Turning slightly to face the long bookshelves, she could make out in the faint light of dawn her father's Locke and Spinoza, Emma Goldman's *Living My Life,* the titles she had read as she passed the bookcase all her life. His desk stood under the window, his papers laid out as if he had just gotten up and might return. Eleanor felt as if his desk, as if all the furniture and the very rooms had been burnished. They shone. She wanted to tell her mother, but when she looked back at Sylvia, she was sleeping, her head laid back on the couch cushions, her mouth slightly open, the beautiful face grown suddenly old. Eleanor stood up, found a soft, green wool blanket, and placed it over her mother. Then she walked upstairs to her old bedroom. Just before she finally slept, she felt her father's love filling the room, then more than the room, the whole sky.

When she got back to New York, Edgar had left a note that he was in his studio, working. She waited for him in his chair, her hands resting in her lap. When he opened the front door, she went to him. She leaned against his soft cotton shirt. He smelled of oil and turpentine. On the wall of the room where they were standing hung one of his drawings from the old days; Eleanor could see it over his shoulder, herself, nude, wearing a straw derby, her long hair falling down her back, sitting on the tangled sheets of their bed.

"I must get back to work," Edgar said finally, patting her back. "I have put off this show for so long. Will you be all right?"

Eleanor nodded and went out to the terrace to search the sky for what she had felt there only days before. But it had returned to its own removed life, empty of human love.

She walked back into the apartment, running her hands along her unused easel, gathering the dust from it on the tips of her fingers, touching her paints. What she had been putting off she felt now was urgent. She had to return to New Mexico. She had to get out, as Teddy would have put it, by the skin of her teeth.

She had fallen in love with Edgar, she guessed later, in what amounted to orchestrated stages. Primed by his reputation, she had been eager to cross his path ever since she arrived in New York. Edgar Stanton, artist, owner of the finest modern gallery in New York, who showed photographers like Eugene Atget and Walker Evans one month and painters like John Marin the next. She met him three days after he had arrived at Miss Barton's School to teach a workshop on drawing (a favor to Miss Wardon; Miss Barton had died in the spring). He was handsome, brisk, authoritative. He strode around the school's neat Turtle Bay park wearing a red vest and a black overcoat. Eleanor's students flocked to him, and paraded into Eleanor's drawing classes breathing Stantonisms: "Sighting! Dürer's device!" At the end of the week, he asked Eleanor to pose for him. He demanded she remain absolutely still as he stood in front of her; his probing eyes were like lenses that never left her face. At the end of the session, as he walked past her, she felt something graze her shoulder—she wasn't sure whether it was his fingertips or his sleeve—and she shivered. She was twenty-three. He was fifty-five.

He asked for and she took him her charcoal drawings. Some of them scared her; she wasn't sure where the shapes had come from. He sat hunched over them in his stark gallery, biting his lower lip.

"I am surprised," he said finally. "This work is completely sincere. You have opened yourself like a flower. "

They saw each other almost every day after that; he often waited for her after her last class and walked with her while she complained of the terrible, uninterested students and her lack of time to paint. He offered to help her, and wrote a letter to one of his patrons on her behalf. The patron wrote back that she could not consider supporting a single woman while she was Edgar's protégé. Edgar tore the letter apart in front of Eleanor's eyes, and they giggled as it fell into the street. He was an odd man; even as young a person as Eleanor could see that. He often covered his mouth out on the street with a stiff linen handkerchief "to keep out the germs." But it was bliss to be his favored companion, to listen to his brilliant thoughts, to be part of his exalted life. Then one day after they had known each other six months, Eleanor received a note from Edgar, sent across town. He was traveling to Italy that day, and would write to her from Florence.

What followed were agonized letters as she sought to understand his sudden disappearance (and to conceal her need to know), and he wrote to mollify and avoid. He was subject to dark depressions, he wrote. Better to keep them from her. Italy always improved his mood.

"Write and tell me that you like me, if only a little," Edgar wrote. "Wait for me. I am afraid you'll go away. Or that otherwise the Fates will ruin me."

He mailed his letter to Eleanor near the Uffizi, on his way to meet an Italian textile heiress.

She wrote that she had been invited to teach at a fine arts school in Cincinnati. He replied, "This may be the end, or near it. Your gift to me was a beautiful mystery, a flame of fire and ice."

Shaken, she withdrew from the job. She all but stopped painting. Instead, she listlessly wandered the streets of Manhattan, reliving their conversations, and the touch of his hand on her skin. When he finally returned, she dressed carefully in a bloodred dress, brushed her long dark hair, and took a cab down to the docks to greet him. Edgar stepped off the gangway and saw a young, austere woman, opening her arms to him. He asked her to marry him on the spot. She hesitated. Edgar laughed anxiously, and fell to his knees.

"What's a man gotta do?"

They were married the following week, at the old courthouse at the tip of Manhattan. Eleanor's cousin Betsy bought her a bouquet of roses and lilies of the valley and stood beside her as the youthful judge read their vows. Teddy sent her a sterling champagne bucket. Sylvia, despite the unorthodoxy of the wedding, was delighted. Her daughter was safe from spinsterhood, and the man was well born. Eleanor felt weak-kneed and grown up, an adult among adults, an artist among artists, her life finally begun.

Their life together settled into a routine. In the mornings Edgar went to his studio, and Eleanor to hers, like two steady draft horses. She painted their domestic life until she had enough work for a show. Edgar hung the paintings with loving care late into the night as she watched from the middle of the empty room. He was thrilled at the reviews, the crowds, the sold-out show; he basked in reflected prominence. His protégé, his wife. At dinner parties, he reveled in the story of how he had "taken" Walker Stern for all he had. After the noise of her fame had died down, they both returned to their working habits. She had loved that time. Now she worked with the figure, a woman model with long, thick blond hair who sat for her while Eleanor discovered how color could make a person's face into a painting. In a few months, she was ready to show Edgar how her work was progressing, and to ask to see his. Standing by the car in the road, she remembered that evening.

She had brought the painting of the woman, a figure dressed in black, seated on a chair, her legs crossed, her hair alive with streaks of light. But before her showing, she asked to see Edgar's work. He was standing at the window, with his hands behind his back, looking at the lights of the Brooklyn Bridge. She was seated, holding her painting wrapped in paper.

He turned. He said quietly that he had not brought anything tonight.

"Why not?" she asked, surprised.

"Because I didn't want to."

"Why?"

"Don't ask me so many questions. Because I did not wish to, that's why."

Eleanor felt unsteady; his look was hard. Finally, she nodded. She did not know what to say.

"So what do you have?"

She unwrapped her painting, her earlier excitement now draining out of her.

He looked at it without a word. He took it up, held it away from him. Her heart pounded in her throat.

"The hair," he finally said. "It's overwhelming her face. And this red"—he pointed to a section of the model's leg—"is not the right shade."

Eleanor felt herself trembling. "But what do you think of the over-all feel of it? I mean, is it working as a concept?"

"Maybe. It's too early to tell. You need to fix quite a lot of it before I could make a judgment." He handed the painting to her and turned back to the window.

"Do you want to dine out tonight or in?" he had asked.

"I don't know," she said. "Are you angry with me, Edgar?"

"Whatever do you mean? Why would I be angry?"

"Your tone, the painting, I don't understand."

"Enough of this nonsense," he said. "Can't the famous Eleanor Garrigue hear a bit of criticism?"

Eleanor had stood up, placed the painting on the table beside her, and walked over to him. She placed her head on his shoulder. "Of course," she said. "I am sorry."

"Apology accepted," he said. "That's my good girl. Now dress yourself up. I think we should go to La Rue's." As she walked away from him, he called to her, "Put on a little rouge. You look too pale."

Eleanor climbed back into the Ford and started the engine.

She parked in the dirt behind the church and made her way to the side entrance. The women had banked someone's early lilacs along with a few hothouse lilies at the altar. The lilacs lifted Eleanor's heart. She genuflected at the pew and sat down, then rose almost immediately to sing the opening anthem, "Christ Our Lord Is Risen Today." The choir processed in, followed by Bill in a chasuble embroidered with gold threads.

"On the first day of the week, at early dawn," Bill read, "the women came to the tomb, taking the spices that they had prepared. They found the stone rolled away . . . While they were perplexed about this, suddenly two men in dazzling clothes stood beside them. The women were terrified and bowed their faces to the ground, but the men said to them, 'Why do you look for the living among the dead?' "

As he read, Eleanor contemplated those women: Mary Magdalene, Joanna, and the woman known only as Mary, the mother of James. They came to the tomb to embalm a body, woman's work. She imagined them getting ready to walk out to the caves, numb with grief, preparing themselves for a painful but familiar job.

She watched the light falling on an acolyte's fair hair. Very suddenly, so suddenly she took in a sharp breath, the story moved into her. This is my story, she said to herself. I, too, look for the living among the dead. And I know why. If I had been with those women, Eleanor thought, I would have wanted to drop my spices and run. Not because I was afraid of those dazzling suits, but because I was afraid of that new life.

"He is not here," Bill read, "but has risen."

Because it was Easter, Eleanor told herself she had to stay, briefly, after the service for the awful church social hour, and found herself captured by Mrs. Stanley, a woman she found adorable in her stiff uprightness. Mrs. Stanley was wearing an Easter hat perched on her head like a fat white chicken laying an egg.

"I've been meaning to tell you, Miss Garrigue," Mrs. Stanley said, leaning toward her conspiratorially, almost sloshing Eleanor's dress with weak tea, the feathers of the hat nearing Eleanor's nose. "Our little committee met last week, and we are pleased to invite you to join the altar guild!"

"Oh, my goodness," Eleanor said. "What an honor."

"I take it your answer is yes, then," Mrs. Stanley said primly.

"Oh, well. No," Eleanor replied, looking around vainly for Bill, whom she finally spied cornered by a man near the parish hall door, with two women hovering nearby.

"No?" Mrs. Stanley said, breathing heavily. She had asthma, was it? Or TB?

"Oh, well—yes, I am afraid. I mean, the answer is no. I can't. I have such little time to paint as it is."

"To paint?"

"Yes, I am a painter."

"Houses?"

"No, paintings."

"Oh."

"Yes."

They fell silent. Eleanor finally extracted herself by complimenting Mrs. Stanley's hat, and practically ran to her roadster. As she drove home, she realized she was speeding, and she slowed down, given her near accident that morning, but soon she was racing along again.

She entered the house and walked quickly down the hall to the bedroom. Leo was sitting up in bed.

"It's Easter," she blurted out. "I had forgotten."

Leo smiled, uncertain. Eleanor felt suddenly awkward. Why had she raced into the room only to stand here, like a schoolgirl?

"How was your, ah, church?" Leo asked.

Eleanor sat down. "I never know exactly what I'm doing there. I mean, I feel afflicted, sometimes, by this need to go." She stopped. She hadn't really talked to anyone about church, except for Bill.

"Would you say you are a religious person?" Leo found he wanted to keep her in the room.

"That's a good question. I don't think so. I mean, I came to it very late. But today it made a little bit of sense to me. Do you know the gospel story that is told at the beginning of Lent?"

"I am afraid not," Leo replied.

Eleanor laughed. "Why would you know it? Right after his baptism in the river, Jesus goes out into the desert, where he is tempted by the devil. Satan asks Jesus why, if he's the son of God, he doesn't change stones into bread."

"That's only vaguely familiar," Leo said.

"I was thinking about it today in church," she said. "That the Resurrection, that Easter, actually, is like changing stones into bread. Only differently from how the devil had in mind. I mean, I think the devil wanted a kind of magic act. And Jesus wouldn't do it. But if you think of Jesus rising from the dead, it's like finding life again, after death. Or, I don't know how exactly to say this, but painting is like that, sometimes. Sometimes you can work and work and work, and nothing goes well, and then suddenly it happens. As if by itself. Stones turn into bread. But it takes an element of, I don't know, seeing, I guess and then grace."

Leo smiled at her. "That is at once very foreign to me and yet very nice," he said. "It's certainly the first time anyone has said anything to me about the resurrection of Jesus that made any sense."

Eleanor grinned. "Oh, Lawdy," she said shyly.

"That is what we were doing," Leo said, almost to himself. "Or maybe the opposite."

"What?"

"How does that story go on? I mean the one about Satan and Jesus?"

"Satan suggests that, if Jesus is the son of God, that he jump from a high tower and God's angels will save him," she replied.

"And?"

"Jesus declines the invitation."

"What happens to Satan?"

"He departs," she said. "The gospel says, 'until another time.' "

"Always until another time," Leo replied.

In the morning, Eleanor looked out the window and saw snow lightly falling. Rita hopped out the door and made round tracks as she trotted across the yard. In a few minutes, she was scratching to be let back in.

"Look outside," Eleanor said to Leo, toweling off Rita's coat. "It's snowing. This place has the most interesting weather. Last year on April second it was seventy degrees."

April second, Leo thought. How did it get to be April second? I've got to act.

"My father used to say no two snowflakes are alike," Eleanor said.

"It's the nature of matter to be asymmetrical," Leo replied.

"What?"

"When the universe was formed, before it was formed, it must have been made of one thing," Leo said. "A thing that was symmetrical, and there must be parts of that still around, somewhere. Or underlying everything. But the rest of it broke up into matter, became diverse, and is asymmetrical."

Eleanor looked at him. He was focused on a place just beyond the bridge of his nose.

"Who are you?"

Leo looked up. She was standing there, her hands hanging helplessly at her sides.

"I wish I could tell you," he said softly.

"I wish you could, too," Eleanor said. She felt suddenly shy. She turned abruptly on her heel and marched out the door. She walked down the hall, her fists jammed into the pockets of her skirt. Reaching for her keys and purse, she called Rita to her side.

"I'm heading into town with the last of the gas," she flung over her shoulder. "Have to check the mail."

The road was paper white ahead of her and the Ford left dark brown tracks behind her, like the lines of a drawing. She tried not to think as she drove—she didn't want to skid again—but she couldn't help returning to the morning conversation: symmetry, asymmetry, what was he talking about? And how did he know about things like that? She didn't understand why she was so awkward with him all of a sudden. It was irritating. She parked at the post office, walked between the cottonwood trees lining the small park in front of it and into the vaulted echoing room. She tried to keep her hope of a letter from Teddy in check as she peered into her box in the banks of boxes that lined the walls like tiny columbariums. Inside, a thin envelope. She fumbled for her key, the little door opened with a squeak, and she pulled out a letter on Edgar's stationery in his neat hand.

Dear Eleanor,

In light of your decision to remain in New Mexico for so many months, I have decided that our situation is untenable. You shall tell me directly when you are returning (an exact date). If I do not hear from you, I will consider coming out there myself to address this crisis, despite the very real risk to my health. The burden is yours. I expect to hear from you shortly.

Yours, E

She looked at the date on the letter. It had been mailed two weeks ago. Her hands shook as she put it into her purse. She turned and made her way out the door and stood in the sun, looking out at the old park.

After that evening when Edgar had critiqued her painting, she had returned to her studio the next morning and placed it on the easel. Betsy was coming over that morning to see what her cousin was up to, as the dear old person put it. Perhaps the red was not the right shade, she thought. Edgar must be right. Eleanor did no work that morning; she simply told herself she must take what Edgar said seriously, find some distance. She paced the studio until Betsy arrived, trailing coats, hats, and packages as if they were loving dogs. As she came in, she saw the painting.

"Oh, Eleanor, my God!" she said.

Eleanor tensed.

"That's quite the most beautiful thing I have ever seen! You have made another great leap. How did you do it?" And she rushed to the painting.

Eleanor, wary, joined her in front of the figure.

Betsy took it off the easel and held it away from her. She put it back.

"Are there more in this series," she asked, "or is this the only one?"

Eleanor, without saying anything, pulled two other canvases from the wall and turned them to face Betsy.

"Oh, Eleanor, these are magnificent," Betsy said. "You have done something here. I so look forward to your show. You and Edgar must have planned it, yes?"

Eleanor felt her tears begin. She shook her head.

"My dear," Betsy said, rushing to her. "Whatever is the matter?"

"Edgar doesn't think they, or it, is right. He says that the color red is off in the leg, that the figure isn't in the right perspective, that . . ." She ticked off the remarks Edgar had made over dinner the night before. "In short," she said, blowing her nose on Betsy's proffered handkerchief, "he doesn't think this one is working. He hasn't seen the others."

Betsy stood back from her. "That is the most awful thing to say," she said finally.

"What?"

"It's absolutely wrong. The great Edgar Stanton may know quite a lot about art, but in this case he's wrong. He's dreadfully wrong. These paintings are magnificent." Betsy walked back to the easel and stared at the first painting. "But what's important is," she said, turning around to face Eleanor, "what do you think?"

"I don't know what to think," Eleanor said miserably. "I can't think." She sank into a chair.

Betsy walked over and stood in front of her. Then she knelt down and grabbed Eleanor's hands. "El, you must believe me. He's wrong. He can't be right about everything. I don't know why he doesn't see it, although I have my . . ." She stopped.

"What?"

"Nothing, really. Nothing. Just believe me. These are beautiful. Keep going."

And Eleanor tried. She worked furiously in the next weeks, shutting out all of the voices in her head: her own old fears, the critics' sharp insinuations, and even Edgar's critique. She worked, and the work finally took over. She felt she was in that reverie of painting where it flowed into her hands, and nothing else mattered. She came home late, dined with Edgar, and fell into bed beside him.

After two months, he asked for a studio visit. She, alarmed, said no. She was not ready yet.

He coaxed. "Come, come, my dear," he said. "Your skin is too thin. Let your old Ed come to see what's up in the painting world of his dove."

And so he came, and walked about the paintings in his dark coat.

She stood in the corner, biting her thumb. There were three now, finished, she thought.

He walked in silence, as was his habit, and then finally he turned to look at her.

"Well, dear heart," he said, "I think that you will need to think on this change of direction, to the figure. It just may not be your strongest suit."

Eleanor felt her heart give way, as if something inside her had been squashed. She rushed from the room.

She lay in bed the next day with a headache and tried not to move. All solicitous, Edgar brought her weak tea and tapioca pudding. He gravely patted her hand. In the afternoon, a note from Betsy arrived, asking for a studio visit the next day.

"Oh, Lord, no," Eleanor said. "I have to put her off." She sent a note back begging her cousin's forgiveness.

In the morning, she rose early and crept out the door to the studio. Her thought was to wipe down the canvases, quickly, before she could stop herself. Destroy the work so she would not have to see it again. The studio was cold in the early morning. Eleanor lit a small fire in the old stove and stood near it, arms wrapped around her chest, staring at the first figure, who calmly looked back at her. Eleanor walked over to the corner of the room where she kept turpentine and rags. She wet a cloth, turned, and advanced on the figure. A knock at the door startled her, and she dropped the rag. Betsy strode in, and behind her Walker Stern, the collector.

"Oh," Eleanor said. "Good morning."

"Good morning, my dear," Betsy said, looking down at the rag on the floor. "I'm sorry to barge in like this, but you've been as hard to find as Judge Crater."

"I am sorry. I did not know you were coming," Eleanor said, and frowned at her cousin.

"I see," Stern said quietly, peering over her shoulder at the painting on the easel. "I thought Edgar had told you I was in town."

Eleanor, surprised, said nothing.

"I am sorry to disturb you," he said, "but I have been waiting for Edgar to call me with an appointment to see you, and I am running out of time. If I might?" He gestured to the easel.

"Of course," Eleanor said, and stepped aside.

He, too, walked around the painting in silence.

"Are there others?" he asked.

"Yes," Eleanor said, trying to keep herself from crying.

She pulled the two other canvases away from the wall and turned them toward her visitors. She heard him suck in his breath.

"Ah," he said. And then, "Miss Garrigue, you have done it. My congratulations."

Eleanor, confused, smiled and murmured a thank-you. Betsy looked triumphant.

"I don't wish to be greedy," he said. "I am sure you and Edgar are planning another show. But the truth is, I would like to purchase these three. You may keep them for the show; I promise I will allow that. I will speak to Edgar, I would think, regarding their price?"

Betsy stepped forward. "No indeed," she said. "You will speak to me. I am representing my cousin in these paintings. Edgar is too busy at the moment with his own work, and I have generously offered to take his place, just for now." She grinned at Eleanor, who was looking at her with alarm.

"But I—" Eleanor began.

"No, no, my dear," Betsy said. "We've talked it all over, remember?"

"How convenient," Stern said. "We can talk immediately, then, if that would suit you? Are you free for lunch, Miss Walcott?"

"Mr. Stern," Betsy said, "in your case, I am always free for luncheon. Allow me to speak to my cousin for a short while privately, and then I will meet you at the Russian Tea Room."

Stern bowed to them both and left the studio.

"What just happened?" Eleanor asked.

"I sold your paintings," Betsy said.

"But you can't. Edgar—"

"Edgar be damned, Eleanor. For some reason he hasn't even returned Walker Stern's calls. He told me on the way over. The man has been calling and calling, begging for a visit. He sent him a note last week."

"He what?"

"He sent Edgar a note. Edgar did not reply. I don't know what's going on, but if I had not run into Mr. Stern at Marie's show yesterday, he would have left town without seeing your work, and have been quite put out as well. I don't know what's going on with your beloved husband, but I took matters into my own hands."

"Edgar will be very angry, Bets. And I am not sure of the paintings. Edgar came to see them again, did I tell you? And he thinks they are all wrong."

Betsy didn't say anything at first. She stood very still. "He's washed up," she said finally. "His show isn't coming along. How long has he been working on it?"

Eleanor stepped back. She could feel the thump of her heart in her chest. "What are you saying, dear cousin?" she said coldly.

"Dearest one, he is hardly working at all," Betsy said. "You come here to work every day. You don't see Edgar out walking the streets while he is supposed to be in his studio."

Eleanor felt something collapsing, as if a building of her father's were slowly falling down.

"He is a great man," she said finally. "He does great work."

"Yes," Betsy said quietly. "That's why you married him, my beloved. And he will again. But for now, you are doing great work, and it is your work we are speaking of."

Eleanor took one hand into the other and sat down. She shuddered as if she had seen a ghost.

"Allow me, darling, to do this," Betsy said firmly. "Let's talk prices."

Eleanor touched the letter inside her purse, straightened her back, and walked back through the snow to the car.

Leo placed his feet on the floor. Steady, he said to himself, steady, like the man says to his horse in the Westerns. He stood and, shivering, grabbed a sweater off the chair near the bed. He walked, one foot in front of the other, until he got to the doorway, and then stopped. He looked down the short hallway as if traversing a border. He could see a glimpse of the living room area, a blanket hanging on a wall, rose and gray, an arrow design. He hesitated, feeling suddenly afraid. He placed one palm against the wall.

As he entered the living room, he saw that this was where she must be sleeping. A bed with low rails of some cheap wood with a light green woven blanket on it. A corner fireplace shaped like a cone, and a small bench built into the wall along one side. On the bench was a collection of round black stones, and, in a square glass box, the white skeleton, he saw as he moved closer, of a coiled snake. The blood floors gleamed. Light filled the room.

In an extension of the living room, the kitchen. Geraniums in a coffee can. A cast-iron pot on the stove. Open shelves without doors. He reached up to one of the shelves and brought down a wood salad bowl with a crack that had been mended with a copper hasp. Everything in this bloody place is primitive, he said to himself. But the plaster walls reminded him of his childhood, those warm rooms with the coved ceilings, the soft white walls you could lean into.

He thought of Einstein and Rosen's theories of separate, parallel universes reached by passing over a bridge. Alice in the Looking Glass, Leo thought. I've fallen through a rabbit hole. I am living not only in another place, but in another time. He looked over at the desk under the window and walked toward it. In this universe, he thought, as he made his way across the room, a woman lives in a house made of mud near a river. Or perhaps I am in London, thinking about the nucleus, the heart of all matter, for fun, for nothing more than fun. Slotin is alive and working in biophysics. And Lotte is still studying chemistry in Prague. I can see her, as if I were on the street outside her window: she is resting her elbows on a desk or standing up to stretch. He stopped himself; if he elaborated this universe, the one in which his life made sense, his heart would break.

He moved his hands over the top of the desk, a solid veneer, crystal desk set, fine pulls made of brass. He hummed a polka to himself as he sat down.

As a boy, Slotin said, he had made tissue-paper fire balloons and piric acid bombs. A vegetarian, he ate eggs every day. Slotin was so kind to Leo, with his proud and stiff manner, his Jewish radar, his locked suitcases. Leo had made no friends in the first month he was on the Project. Slotin discovered Leo's love of cigars and found him a dozen Cuban Montecristos. Together they took them to the hospital and asked to use an x-ray machine for secret work, to find out if radiation changed the taste of tobacco.

Leo told him his favorite poem was the tragedy of the Madach, in which Adam, with Lucifer as his guide, travels the world and sees the end of the world coming, caused by human greed and violence, the only survivors a few Eskimos in a landscape of ice.

"That's a grim tale," Slotin had said.

"It has a narrow margin of hope," Leo had replied. "That's all I require."

In this reverie, Leo, almost without realizing it, pulled open one of the wide front drawers of the desk and found what he had been looking for since he got up from the bed: a stack of clean white stationery in a pale box. He took a look at the rest of the drawer's contents, a handwritten letter on a yellow legal pad with a scrawled signature; a box of paper clips; an interview from *The New York Times* with the president of Czechoslovakia, Tomáš Garrigue Masaryk; postcards from a museum in New York; a list of books, including one on painting. Amazing, Leo thought to himself. So she might be related indeed to Charlotte Garrigue Masaryk. What were the odds on that? Under the clipping was a photo. Leo picked it up. A man with a thatch of thin short hair, round glasses, a white brush mustache. An older man but still handsome, a wry, seductive, and secret look in the eyes, and next to him, a younger woman—yes, Eleanor—in a white dress carrying a bunch of roses with ribbons, staring up at him, like a flower bending toward the sun. Leo held the photograph for a few seconds, and then he put it back in the drawer.

He wet a finger with his tongue and lifted a sheet out of the drawer and set it on the green blaze of the blotter. In the rounded crystal well was a pool of black ink. A wreath of leaves was etched along the sides of the heavy square stopper. Resting on the green blotter was a blue enameled fountain pen. He stopped. What to say, exactly? The man who read this letter would have about two minutes. He wrote a line. He rested his chin on his palm. Then he heard a noise and didn't understand what it was until part of him understood and he slammed the drawer shut. A door had opened. His heart jammed his throat. A figure stepped into the room, nearly six feet tall, wearing a long black dress and a hat decorated with plastic red roses and sunflowers. He tried to smile, wave a hand in greeting. Griefa stalked over and stood, hands on her hips, looking down at him.

"Who are you?" she demanded. *"Donde está Señora Garrigue?"*

"I don't speak Spanish," Leo said, in German. Then, realizing his mistake, he said, "Miss Garrigue is not at home."

"Señora Garrigue no está aquí?" Griefa said softly, and placed her large hand on his right wrist.

Leo gestured with his chin toward the bedroom, mimed a headache with his left hand, and started to stand up. Griefa held him down. He fumbled with his hand on the desk. Something is wrong with him, she thought. She noticed the bedding on the railed couch made in Taos.

"Please," Leo said. "Don't tell anyone." He met her eyes. I will tell whom I like, she thought, and nodded. Does he think that she would gossip all over town about her employer? Gringo men are fools.

"Antes de hablar es bueno pensar," she said to him. *Before you speak, it's always good to think.* And, deciding he was harmless, she turned toward the bedroom.

Leo sat helpless at the desk.

He did not look up when Eleanor entered the room. What she saw, for an instant, was a form at her father's desk, wearing his sweater. For a moment, he was her father, and she couldn't move.

Then Leo heard the whisper of her feet against the floor. He slipped the sheet of paper under the blotter, turned, and before she could speak, he put his fingers to his lips.

"Is that sound a cricket?" he asked.

She listened. "Yes," she replied.

"I had one once," he said, quickly, trying to calm and distract her. "I kept it in a little bamboo cage beside my bed. Just overnight. My nurse explained that we did not know what they ate. I suggested porridge."

Eleanor slowly sat down in the nearby rocking chair.

Leo noticed that on her right wrist she wore a thin silver bracelet with a small square tawny stone.

Eleanor was about to ask him how he had walked in here, but instead she said, "The first day I spent here, before I got Rita, I was so in need of company, I caught a little horned toad and kept him in a bowl by the bed."

Leo cocked his head. He felt suddenly light.

"Companionship," he said. He thought of his grandfather warding off the evil eye by adding the Yiddish word *kaynahorah* after speaking of good health or happiness and almost said it here, feeling his luck changing. He remembered his grandfather walking toward him through a beech forest, yellow leaves raining from the trees behind him.

Eleanor smiled, and then found herself looking at his hands, which were resting on his lap. They were square. On one hand, the little finger was crooked, as if it had been broken long ago. Sitting in a chair, rather than lying in bed, made him more of a person, less a patient. She felt the odd shyness she had felt earlier coming back, but she didn't give in to it. Instead, she looked up from his hands and into his eyes.

"Eleanor," he said. And Griefa's broom crashed against the chair in the bedroom.

"Have you met Griefa?" she asked, alarmed.

"I believe that I have," Leo replied, and laughed. His first laugh in how many months.

"Would you like her to wash your shirt?" she asked, and thought, Oh, stupid, stupid thing to say.

"I would be honored," Leo replied. He saw her blush. He did not want her to move. "I would also be delighted to wash myself." He stood up, one step after another, crossed toward her, and when he got to the place in front of her, he leaned down to look at her eyes. Green, he thought. They are green. She looked up at him, and Griefa walked into the room.

Eleanor turned. "Griefa," she said, "this is—"

"Leo," he said to Eleanor, and then moved toward Griefa to shake her hand. "Just Leo for now."

Griefa told him to go into the bathroom and take a bath and take off his clothes and hand them to her, in as many words. He obeyed. As she walked back out into the living room, her arms full of laundry, she took in Eleanor, who was still sitting in the rocker with her hand resting on one shoulder.

"Donde menos se piensa," Griefa said, *"salta la liebre."*

Eleanor smiled. She stood up and walked to the desk to look out at the hills. Then she looked down and saw a tip, a sliver of white. She pulled on the corner, the sheet slid smoothly from under the blotter, and she read, "Dear F—Pass this, please, urgent to R." She read it again. "Dear F." She sat down. "Dear F—Pass this, please." She looked up from the sheet at the distant and silent mountains. He wanted to pass something to someone, but he had nothing to pass, at least nothing on him that she had seen. Nothing, she thought, except information.

Eleanor heard a voice, and realized he was singing in the bathtub. She clutched her arms around her chest. Who is he? No last name. Her slip slid against her breasts.

Griefa walked back into the room. "Señorita Eleanor," she said, "what clothing can I give him while I wash his own?"

Eleanor, startled, turned. "That's a good question," she said. "Give him my bathrobe for now." And impulsively she took Leo's laundry from Griefa and looked in the shirt for a label. It had been expertly cut out. The khaki pants were made by Brooks Brothers. Who is he? She realized she was holding her breath. She had been crazy to allow a strange man to live in her house for so long, and she must run, immediately, to find help. Because the one profession she had not thought of was obvious, in a man who spoke German when delirious and wrote a letter about passing something to someone else—that of spy. Christ, she thought. He lied to me.

She looked up and saw him watching her from the door of the bathroom, wearing her flannel robe.

Why is she inspecting my clothes? Leo thought as he leaned against the door, the feeling of calm and pleasure from the bath slowly draining out of him. She has a right, he said to himself. But why so suddenly after what had happened between them? Is she

going to turn him in? Now? He couldn't see—her body was block-
ing it—the sheet of paper on the desk. Eleanor turned and slid the
letter—for it is a letter, now it is named—back under the blotter and
turned around.

She nodded at him, a nod from a stranger, put down his clothes,
and walked out of the room. Leo stood at the bathroom door, thinking, calculating. He told himself that what had happened between
them had not happened; it had happened to him, not to her, and now,
for some reason, she was a stranger again. She was even more than a
stranger: she was an enemy. He felt his heart pound.

Eleanor thought the best thing to do was to quickly, quickly go
back to town and find Bill. She prayed she would not run out of gas.

Leo heard her leave the house, and the engine of the Ford starting
up. He had no clothes. He felt himself completely alone, and then he
saw the square of the green blotter and began to think again. He
tried to imagine what it looked like as he stood up and crossed to her.
He tried to imagine the desktop and realized that he hadn't checked
it. Then he understood what had happened as he lay innocent in the
bath, singing his nurse's old lullaby. But why had she not simply
asked him? Griefa came into the room and saw him, and she heard
the car leaving the driveway. They stood as if frozen in a child's
game, and then she picked up his clothes and handed them to him.
She then walked out to her wagon and returned with an old jacket.
He looked at the clothes as if they were alien objects, and then he
slowly went back into the bathroom and closed the door.

Eleanor drove with Rita sitting on the seat beside her. The thoughts
that flew through her mind could not be called even thoughts, but
pieces, chunks of light. She remembered his eyes, and the way they
flooded her with light and pleasure, and then she saw the letter. I am
a fool, she thought. Always naive. I should have taken him to the hospital. Eleanor cried, one tear at a time, as if they were eking out of

her eyes. He lied to me, she thought. He probably lied to me about everything. And I, as usual, swallowed it, hook, line, and sinker. She stopped crying. She parked outside the church rectory and ran up the short sidewalk and knocked on the door.

Leo dressed in his shirt and pants and the jacket Griefa had given him; the jacket was covered in plaster and mud. He tried to think. If he left this house, he would have to walk somewhere. To a hotel? He could make his way to a hotel and wire the Met Lab, but he would have to go to a telegraph office and then someone would know. If he could get the letter mailed . . . He opened the door of the bathroom and Griefa was standing there, in the little hall. She looked at him and laughed. He looked down at his pants and saw the fly was unbuttoned, and he turned around and buttoned it, and when he turned back, she was holding out a piece of cheese and a tortilla. He motioned to her, went back into the bedroom, retrieved his money belt, then returned to the desk. He reached under the blotter, took out the letter and an envelope, and then Griefa was pushing him out the door. He stood outside in the gathering snow, and stuffed the cheese into his pocket. He felt weakened by more exercise than he'd had in a month at least, and walked out the gate.

Bill sat listening to Eleanor. He heard, A man by the river. Wet legs. In the house. Over the last week and a half. A Czech, or possibly, terribly, a German. A letter. The name, Leo. A sister in a camp. No doctors.

"Bill, do you know German?"

"Yes," he replied.

"He said something over and over in his sleep, at the beginning, when I first found him. He kept repeating it with great urgency. I finally wrote it down. It must be German. It was like 'Rouse ous dem fo-ee-er. Rouse ous dem fo-ee-er!' "

He handed her a cup of tea. Outside the sky was growing darker.

"I'm not sure, of course, but it does sound like German. It would be 'Get out of the fire.' "

"I don't know where that gets us."

"Tell me the wording of the letter again," he said.

"It was simple," Eleanor said. She visualized the words on the page. "Dear F—Pass this, please, urgent to R."

Bill pondered. The room was getting colder, and he got up and threw a piece of pinion wood on the fire.

"I don't think I know anything about spies," he said. "A friend of mine helped make a short movie for the army about Sargent Snafu. It's about how there are Japanese and German spies everywhere, even hidden in moose heads over a bar, as I recall. I'd better come out there with you, don't you think?" he said. "Or do you want to go to the police?"

"Oh, no, not the police," she said hastily, and Bill wondered why not, but by then he was getting up and putting on his coat.

"It's really snowing," he said, and she nodded, and then they were out the door.

When they arrived at her house, the snow had capped the adobe walls of her garden like soft fur edging and a deep silence filled the river basin. She saw that the gate was open and Griefa's wagon was gone. Inside, the room was still. She rushed into the bedroom and saw the empty bed. She walked back into the living room where Bill was standing at the desk, holding the stamps tray, and she said, "He is gone."

"Ah," Bill said.

Eleanor sat down on the couch and put her head in her hands. She was crying. Why is she crying? Bill wondered, but he pushed that thought aside.

"I had begun to like him," she whispered, and Bill felt a jolt near his heart.

"Ah," he said.

"Would you like a glass of something?"

"Yes," he said. "Do you have whiskey?"

"Neat or with ice?"

"Neat."

He sat, running his hands over his thighs.

She handed him the glass. He sipped. She lit the fire. The snow was coming down thickly now, a wet spring snow.

"What would be around here to spy on?" she asked.

"Nothing, really," Bill replied, trying to think back on anything he had heard that made sense other than vague rumors. "Someone said something about electric rockets once. He'd heard it in a bar." And then he thought of David. Early on David had said something about "war-related work." Where does David work? He had never asked, prettily keeping away from something David was obviously not comfortable talking about.

Eleanor was looking out the window.

"Maybe what he said was true," he said to her. "Maybe he was camping and got lost. Maybe the letter is nothing more than, than . . ." But he couldn't explain it.

"That's the trouble," she said. "I can't make sense of it."

Then she suddenly got up and walked past him to the desk. She slid her hand under the blotter.

"It's not there," she said. "It's not there." It took Bill a moment; then he understood.

She sat down again.

"I cannot imagine what to do," she said.

Slowly, in the back of Bill's mind, a plan was forming, a way to help, a way to act. He sipped his whiskey.

"I think I may be able to do something," he said. "I think I may know someone who can shed some light."

She looked up, and he saw the relief on her face. I can help her, he thought. I can be of help to her.

He looked at his watch. The snow was falling in thick blankets. "I'd better go," he said. "I will see you tomorrow. Get some rest. Sleep well. Would you like to pray?"

"Yes," she said.

Bill bowed his head: "O loving Father, keep watch over your servant Eleanor. And keep watch, dear Lord, with those who work or watch or weep this night, and give your angels charge over those who sleep. All for your love's sake. Amen."

As he was going out the door, he stopped. "Are you worried?" he said, thinking suddenly of the stranger out there near the house. "Would you like to come into town?"

"No," Eleanor said. "I have Rita here. I will be all right."

"Good night, then," he said, and shut the door behind him. As he drove the rutted road back toward the lights of Santa Fe, he turned the problem over and over in his mind.

I will see David next week as usual, he said to himself. Or I could send him a note sooner. I will talk to him about this mysterious man at Eleanor Garrigue's house. Perhaps he will know something. Maybe I should just go to the police. Do the police handle spies?

Eleanor stoked the fire, and then went to the kitchen and pulled a jar of spaghetti sauce out of the refrigerator. She did not notice that her hoarded cheese was missing. She poured herself another glass of whiskey. She set the table for one. As the water for the spaghetti was heating, she sat at the table, lit a candle, and said the words of the prayer over in her mind. She found she was thinking of the man whose name was Leo, out in the cold, and praying for him.

SEVEN

Bill cleaned the sacristy methodically, placing the corporals in their square stacks and the purificators in their longer folds. He ran his hands along the fair linen. Mrs. Stanley took each piece, smudged with lipsticks or dappled with wine, home on Sunday afternoon and hand-washed them using what was called French laundry water. Bill had a fantasy of water carried carefully in small vials in locked cases from France and then distributed at great expense to altar guild women lined up at midnight in New York Harbor.

He had recently realized that he liked the Holy Ghost more than he did God the Father. The Holy Ghost was a Comforter, the Book of Common Prayer said, and Bill always thought of Him as a down-filled quilt. The Holy Ghost is always around, Bill thought, brooding over creation (as Genesis had it), unlike the creator who makes an appearance now and then, makes a world, harangues prophets from burning bushes, procreates a son, then disappears for another thousand years. A fan of the grand gesture. The Holy Ghost, on the other hand, is the God of small, ordinary acts, making of daily imperfection, a saving grace. Bill whistled. At last, he thought. I see how I can be of help to Eleanor. How interesting that it has come about because of a mysterious stranger. How these things happen!

If we are the guests, then the Holy Ghost is our Innkeeper, Bill thought as he tidied the little room. He imagined the Holy Ghost rummaging around for just the right brand of tea, or a pair of nice wool socks. Dusting, mopping, mending. Making lunch. Giving us just enough to make us capable of the next step. Bill recited to himself the last lines of Gerard Manley Hopkins's "God's Grandeur," memorized not at seminary but at a poetry library he had stumbled on in lower Manhattan: *"Because the Holy Ghost over the bent/World broods with warm breast and with ah! bright wings."* He thought of the great saints: Theresa of Avila, on such good terms with God that when her cart was frozen in mud in northern Spain she shook her fist at Him and said, If this is how you treat your friends, it is no wonder you have so few of them. The virgin martyrs: banned, burned, eviscerated. And even my beloved Francis, Bill thought, who kissed a leper on the mouth and understood that everything was upside down; even he doesn't seem so useful to me, in the end.

It's more like one simple act after another, a chain of acts. He wondered how it had been for Eleanor to take care of this man in her house, alone out there in the countryside. She must have been afraid—how terrible for her, with no protector nearby.

"We thank ye all our God with hearts and hands and voices," Bill sang, as he polished a chalice that had a small cross on its cup. What is silver polish made of? he wondered.

Bill rinsed the chalice under the tap, washed his hands, and took a final look around. He walked down the aisle of the little church, waving to the cherubs in one of the windows. At the rectory, he wrote a brief note to David, suggesting an earlier day for chess, perhaps Saturday morning? He addressed the envelope: Box 1616, Sandoval County, then looked at it and thought, That is such an odd address.

He allowed himself a bit of fantasy regarding Eleanor. He could help her with this situation, whatever it was. He would then appear to her as a man rather than a thing dressed up in a little mortician-like suit or her spiritual teacher, whatever it was she saw him as. He could help her, and then she'd look at him differently. Faith was really so simple, he said to himself this morning. You waited until the right moment, and then all of your preparations and prayers paid off, the way flowers bloomed in a well-tilled garden.

He looked out the window and, as if he had conjured her, there she was. Eleanor, looking rather odd, it seemed to him, arriving on his doorstep. He took a look at himself in the mirror, quickly. Smoothed his beard, practically pinched his cheeks. He noted that he had made enough coffee this morning for two. He tugged open the heavy door before she had time to knock, and was about to greet her a hearty good morning and invite her in when she overrode him.

"I have made a mistake," she said. "I think we'd better keep him a secret for now."

Bill looked at her face, and specifically at her eyes.

"Come in," he said. "Do come in. I have a wonderful little pastry that I can't eat by myself, and I've made a fine cup of coffee." He opened the door to her, and gestured with what he hoped was gallant ease.

"Oh, no, I can't," she said. "I need to get back. I need to try to find him."

Bill was suddenly furious. Why in heaven's name did she need to get back? He felt awkward, clumsy, and he said, curtly and tightly, "Well, let me know if there is anything I can do," and he turned his back to her. He looked at his own living room as if looking at a museum, an old shoddy place with dust on the shelves and cobwebs in the corners, which just minutes ago had been full of light and promise. He turned around to say something to her, to apologize, to try to speak to her again, but she was out the gate. Not even a wave.

He stood at the door like an idiot, and then he turned, picked up the letter to David, and walked out in the cold air. The sky was a deep blue; snow covered the grass and the tree limbs. The snow had weighted a branch of a willow so that it formed a bow. He stepped into the tracks of someone else's feet on the sidewalk, walked past the small doors of the stores that lined Palace Avenue; the cotton-woods were beginning to bud out, the snow was melting on the patched adobe walls. He stepped into the post office, greeted the mistress there, who was giving some poor tourist the wrong direc-tions to Taos, and let the letter slide in.

EIGHT

In the days that followed, Bill waited for a reply from David on tenterhooks. He didn't want to go too far in thinking about it, but he felt a keenness about this appointment for a chat with David, a man he wasn't even sure he liked, that was like that of a lover waiting for a rose-scented note. He went to the post office the next day, in the early afternoon, as soon as the mail arrived. Nothing. Then, on the second day of his waiting, a few lines saying yes, it was fine, they could meet on Saturday. On the walk back to the rectory, Bill was as excited as he used to be as a child at the expectation of a long-desired toy. Just as he walked into his office, he also felt a wave of what felt like dread, but this floated so quickly and almost delicately through him that he banished it. Later, he would remember that moment, and the curious mixture of dread and frenzy, and how it should have taught him something about faith and destiny, those two things he thought he knew so much about.

He arrived at La Fonda early. He'd eaten a bad, overpriced cinnamon roll and drunk a not bad cup of Nuveco when David walked in, looking neither to the left nor right, like an angry bear. Lydia arrived at the table. Bill said pleasantly to her that she never seemed to have a day off. She ignored him and asked David what he wanted. David snorted that he wanted coffee, of course.

"I am sorry to take you away from your weekend," Bill began.

"I don't have much of a weekend," David replied.

"Will you be going to Albuquerque?"

"No," David said simply.

He said nothing more, and so Bill launched in.

"David," Bill said, "I know that you and I have not talked about your work, and I am aware that it's war-related and probably secret in some way or another, but I had a question for you." He stopped. He had thought this through, but somehow he couldn't remember exactly how he was going to say it. "I have a friend, a parishioner actually, who has found someone beside the Rio Grande. He may have had some kind of accident. And we were wondering if it was possible that you might know him, or know who he is, because he has a foreign accent. And I think he might have come from the mesa where . . . well, you know the rumors in town."

Bill looked up. David was playing with his spoon.

"A friend of yours has found someone by the river?"

"Yes," Bill said.

"I don't know what that has to do with me," David said. Lydia asked David if he wanted a refill, and he practically pushed her away with his hand. "No."

"I thought," Bill said, "that where you work, you might know people, other people. I don't know."

"What is his accent? From where? Be concise."

Bill, offended and yet wishing to please, said, "Well, she isn't sure, but maybe German or possibly Czech."

"German or Czech?" asked David, and pushed his hand against the table. "Are you sure?"

"No," said Bill. "I have not myself heard him speak. Nor met him, for that matter." He frowned. Back in his mind, he began to wonder why he was talking to David at all, when, let's be clear on this, Eleanor said he need not. Not in so many words, that is, because she had not known what he planned, but basically she said . . . what did she say? Something about how it was all right, that she had made a mistake. So why am I here? Bill asked himself. Because I thought it wise. I thought it would be good to make sure, to find out, and to protect her. She may not know, really, that she has made a mistake. After all, this is a stranger, found beside a river. And he felt better.

"Well," David said, "this really has nothing to do with me." He was standing up. "Thanks for the coffee," he said. "I will see you as usual on Wednesday."

"Certainly," Bill said. He felt uncomfortable, off balance. Then he remembered.

"Oh, David," he said, calling out. "I forgot something."

David stopped and turned. Several people at other tables looked up. Bill smiled apologetically, at them, in general, and at David. David walked back.

"He said his name was Leo."

"Leo?"

"Yes," Bill said. "Foolish of me to forget. Leo something. He didn't give his last name."

"I see," David said. "A German or a Czech named Leo." He was smirking, Bill realized. "As I said, not much I can do." And he turned and was gone.

Bill sat at the table alone. Lydia poured him more coffee, but he didn't lift his cup. His first thought was that he'd been cheated. David was supposed to have said he'd come to the right place. And what? That he would look into whether someone was missing where he worked. It was supposed to have gone simply and smoothly, with Bill cast as hero and David as his lieutenant. The hero would then return to the maiden, bearing the good news, and she would look up at him, gratitude and adoration written on her face. He wiped his mouth and stood up, almost colliding with Lydia, who was standing very close by.

"I'm sorry," he said to her.

She nodded her head.

David worked steadily in the shop, wrestling with making the molds. He had rehearsed how to say it, how to ask it, how to appear so casual as to be not very interested in the answer.

Kistiakowsky arrived, and they talked about the recent cracks in the molds. After a pause, David said, "I haven't seen Dr. Simms lately, or Dr. Stark."

A silence. Kistiakowsky said, "Dr. Simms has taken a brief vacation."

David looked up and smiled. "Oh," he said. "Where? I was going to ask him if he wanted to play chess again."

Another silence. "I think he went down to Albuquerque." Then Kistiakowsky turned on his heel and left. David pondered the rumor that had started a few weeks ago. Slotin and Kavan and their assistant had suddenly left Tech Area A. A nurse saw two men at the hospital. David had not seen Slotin or Kavan since then. The student who had worked with them had been seen leaving the Project in a car driven by a staff sergeant. Kistiakowsky had not said a word about Slotin. David poured the Baratol into a new mold. He measured the wax, poured another mixture, and cooled it in the refrigerator. He checked the molds for cracks.

Was it possible that the man the priest was describing was Leo Kavan? It seemed unlikely; he was probably just a man with an accent. I'll bet he comes from Florida, David thought. No one out here is used to an accent other than Mexican. But the priest said he was Czech. Dr. Kavan is Czech. But who among these people would know? Could there have been an accident? That was not a word allowed on the Project. "There will be no accidents," Groves had said in an early speech. But if there had been one, it would explain why Kavan was not around, and Kistiakowsky's reluctance to talk. Not because Kavan had disappeared and someone had found him wandering around near the river. But suppose it was Kavan? Then what? How could this be of use to us? It was tantalizing.

He walked out into the afternoon sun to take a brief break. The lab was always hot and stuffy and filled with the smell of chemicals. He was always surprised at the sun when he walked out, at the glare.

NINE

In what seemed like minutes after Leo had walked out Eleanor's gate, the snow had begun to fall in earnest. He had stood there, not having much idea of where he was going, and then had said to himself that he must simply move—there was nothing else to do— and hope that he would find his way into town. How far, after all, could it be? But he had not counted on the snow. It fell in wet flakes and piled in front of him. He looked up and could not see the sky. He had thought he would follow the road, simply put one foot in front of the other and walk into town, but soon it was hard to make out the way. He had only the light jacket of some crude fabric, layered in dirt and plaster. That woman—Griefa? Her husband or brother must be a worker of some kind, Leo thought. What a strange woman, he thought to himself, and yet she seemed to trust him. Unlike Eleanor Garrigue. How had he been so stupid as to think—but here he stopped himself. He hugged his arms to his chest and plodded forward. The radiation illness and time in bed had left him weak. He had been a strong man before that, boxing in the gymnasium three times a week, but now he was slow and hesitant.

He was not even sure he was on the road anymore, and seeing a large pinion to his left, Leo made for it, hoping that underneath its branches it might be drier or warmer. He sat down in the dry needles under the arms of the old tree, his arms folded across his chest, trying to remember how you make a fire using two sticks. His hands were numb. He considered the irony of his position: world-renowned physicist dies of hypothermia in a desert wasteland, could not remember how to make a fire. He felt his stubborn hope diminishing. The encounter with Eleanor that afternoon had taken it out of him. He had not realized, until he looked into her eyes—and yes! she had looked back—how numb he had been, how careful not to allow any feeling other than determination into his heart. For that brief time, while he lay in the bath, he had felt like a man, in the world, human. He had soaped his body, thinking of her slim wrists and her dark hair, her strong shoulders under her white shirts. A woman painter. Paint on her fingers. Canvases against the wall. The one bright painting in the bedroom.

He blinked, and realized he'd been asleep. Shaken, Leo stood up and hopped up and down. If I fall asleep, I really will die, he thought, and started out from under the tree. The snow was falling less heavily, and he found his way back to the ruts that marked the road.

He was looking at a white landscape that stretched out in front and around him without break. The small twisted trees grew here and there, and the rounded bushes with pale yellow flowers now caked with snow. He could see nothing: no buildings, no walls, nothing bigger than the pinion trees except for a few rocky outcroppings. He had not really been anywhere else in this bloody country since his arrival, he realized, besides what they called the Hill, the pueblo just below it, and Eleanor's house. It seemed to be largely flat around here, with a few hills and the oblong tableland in the distance, what the half-days called a mesa. At the foot of one of the hills was a row of taller, leafy trees now burdened with snow. Leo tried to remember their names. One foot in front of the other. Lamb. Wool. Cotton. Cottonwoods. Named for the swirls of white fiber that their seeds released in the spring.

The snow was thick and wet. Every now and then as he walked, the snow leaked into the top of one or the other of his low boots. It melted into the top of his socks and made its way down. Cold and now wet feet.

He thought of the many hotel rooms he had lived in, the men who worked at the desks, the one in Chicago who had a memory, he'd said, "like a steel trap."

He patted the letter in his coat pocket, which Felix might deliver for him. It was what he lived for at this moment. Life's meaning, he had learned, was found in deeds. He turned over in his mind again how to phrase the rest of it.

"Please exercise your power as commander in chief . . . to rule that the United States shall not . . ." Or maybe "in the present phase of the war, the United States shall not . . ."

He realized he had stopped. Must not stop, he told himself, but he did not move. His mind fogged with despair. No use, it said, no use. He shook himself. He looked up and saw a tree some distance away. I will get to that tree, he said. He realized he had said it out loud. That tree, the bent pinion in the snow. He walked along the rut, and missed seeing the hump of snow underneath which was a rock. He fell forward, crying out in surprise, his ankle twisted around the rock, his bare hands skidding into the dirt under the snow. He felt tears on his face. Must get up.

He stood up, brushed the snow off his clothes, placed his hands in his pockets, and waited until the pain in his ankle subsided enough to move forward. It hurt to walk, but he could still manage it. He would still manage it. He got to the tree. There he rewarded himself. Good. You got to the tree. But standing still brought the cold into his bones. He thought of hopping, but the ankle stopped him. He waved his arms and flapped them against his ribs. He looked up the road. He could see a rock ahead, red with white patches, a crystal of some kind. He realized the snow had stopped falling. Only a few flakes spiraled down out of the gray sky. He thought for the first time about how far snowflakes must fall. From a cloud layer, thousands of feet, how many thousands? He thought of the structure of a snowflake, the things that are asymmetrical, and the search for the few things that are not. He blinked. He had slept again, this time standing up. Fear shot into his stomach. He could not, could not sleep. He stomped his feet, and pain flew up his leg from his ankle; he swore. The rock was the next goal. He would get there, to that rock. He started walking, the snow wet and soft under his feet. Some mud appearing in patches along the ruts. Red mud, white snow. He decided to make himself remember. The old Cavendish lab. His friend Guy, lounging across the table, an Imperial cigarette held rakishly in one hand while he gestured toward the blackboard.

"See here, you stupid Czech, there is a way. We can use paraffin wax instead of lead."

The bathtub near Trafalgar Square, the big white enamel tub with the lumpish square feet, no fancy claws here. Soaking in the morning, all morning—there was no better place to think than a bath. The maid would come to the door every hour to ask if he was all right. Neutrons were better than alpha particles for bombarding nuclei.

He got to the rock and placed a hand against it as if touching home base in a child's game of hide-and-go-seek. He looked up the road and saw a tree, this one low and round, rather like a cypress from his youth when the family had gone to the seashore for bathing. He tried not to think of his youth. Hidden among his memories, he realized, was an irritant, a faint scraping at the edge of his consciousness, something that had always been there, in the dark, but dislodged by the accident, set free to float, as if a bit of moss had been loosened from the bottom of a lake.

He had thought, all this time, that he was working on the gadget— no, here in the snow alone, he would call things as they were: the bomb. He had told himself that he worked on the bomb for the sake of Lotte, to blow the Germans to kingdom come, whatever the risk to the world. And, of course, because the Germans were working on the bomb themselves. He had wanted to end their awful sense of a right to dominate, their pitiless arrogance. He had pictured more than once Hitler being blown to bits, and been surprised by the amount of pleasure it gave him. But here in the snow, leaning against this cold ancient rock on this long empty road, freezing, he realized the lie he had told himself.

Without his contribution, they simply would not be where they were. He remembered Fermi looking up at him when he had said "chain reaction," and the light in that handsome face. Being part of the brightest group of men ever assembled, and more than any of that, being part of something so large, so completely—he almost laughed at the innocence of the word that came to his mind to describe the Project—so completely practical.

No more theory, no more working in space. No, this had a real object, a real goal, as real as the rock under his hand. They would actually put all of the theory to use and find out if it really worked. Make a material object, a practical military weapon. And this weapon would . . . His mind went blank, muddled. Keep going, whispered a part of his thoughts, keep going. It would destroy whole cities at once, and kill hundreds of thousands of people. They would die exactly as . . . Leo stopped.

He had worked on the bomb because he had enjoyed it. He had liked the science, and the camaraderie, and the solving of problems one by one. He had seen his theory made real and he had reveled, finally, in the power it gave him. Until he had seen, just precisely, what was to come, what would be unleashed, what would fly from the box they had opened.

He made for the tree. The sky was darkening, the light was fading. Night. Panic rose in his throat. If he didn't get somewhere by night, then he was really done for. He felt furious all at once. That he would have gotten himself into what the Americans called . . . what was it, a jelly? A pickle, one of them said. Why a pickle? No, a jam. He had gotten himself into a jam, having pulled himself out of much worse situations; he was going to die of the cold on a dirt road in a place so unnoticed by the world that you could build a bomb there that could very well blow everything up. He wondered to himself if they had built the tower at the test site. He had looked at a map carefully when he first arrived. Not much in the south. A long stretch of desert down there, low mountains, flat areas. A few villages. No real city until you got to El Paso, Texas. Good place to detonate a bomb and close your eyes.

They would have had to solve several problems first. He wondered how they were doing. The old sense of purpose came back to him, briefly. Had they solved the purely mechanical problems? The cracks in the molds? Had they tested the theory of the empty core, the falling spike? It would take a while to move everything south, to the test place. It would have to be not too far from the Hill, so they could get everything down there in a day at the most. They might be transporting men even now, and the thing itself, the core. God, he thought, how are they going to move that?

"In cotton swaddling," Slotin had said. "Wrapped like a babe in the manger."

That morning, Slotin had greeted him with a slap on the back. His narrow boy's face full of light and promise, frozen in Leo's memory. Leo will always see Slotin standing in front of him, his white lab coat open, his hands in his pockets, making a joke about the mud.

They began the experiment. The idea was to move two hemispheres toward each other on a rod, to allow them to reach only the first step, and then separate them, so as to avoid, as Slotin used to say, "a little accident."

Slotin was moving the two half-moons together with screwdrivers.

The counter ticked and the red signal lamps were blinking. Leo was behind him. Writing on the board with a chalk.

A screwdriver fell to the floor; the meter stopped. Leo heard the silence first; he half turned. The room was filled with blue light. Leo yelled, *"Raus aus dem Feuer!"* to Slotin. As he screamed, he saw out of the corner of his eye that the lights had stopped flickering. They were glowing, a bead of red. *Get out of the fire!* But Slotin leaned forward, and with his bare hands separated the hemispheres to keep them from reaching critical mass, saving Leo, the assistant, the room, the lab, and the city, and sacrificing himself.

Leo heard himself shouting. Slotin turned, slowly, and with great courtesy told Leo to be quiet, please. The assistant was standing by the door. Slotin told them both to stand still, not to move, please. He walked to the chalkboard and drew their positions, estimating their distance from the assembly. He looked over his shoulder at Leo.

"What do you think?" he said. "Seven feet?" Leo nodded, his head feeling like a balloon made of tissue, like one of Slotin's paper balloons.

Slotin said, "So they will know how much you got."

Leo watched Slotin write. His hand was already turning red.

"Okay," Slotin said, and then he turned and the three of them walked outside. They sat down beside the muddy road. Leo looked across at one of the green buildings. It was as if the whole town had gone silent. Leo could think of nothing to say. Then Slotin turned to him and said, "You will come through all right."

He patted his arm. Leo nodded. Then Slotin said, this time with a second of catch in his voice, "But I haven't the faintest chance myself."

The car came to take them to the hospital. Leo waited for Slotin to climb in. They sat in the back seat. The driver kept asking if they were comfortable. He was a young GI. His face was sweating. Slotin said to him to calm down. At the hospital, two nurses were waiting, and they rushed to the door, opened it, and tried to help Slotin out. Slotin pushed their hands away. He turned to Leo. He said, "I have been glad to have known you," and then he stood up and walked with the nurses inside.

There was no funeral for Slotin. No one spoke of him in the labs on the Hill. Every part of his history, the details of his short life, had been erased.

It was as if he had, one day, disappeared.

Leo had a metallic taste in his mouth. He got to the tree, and rested. Two minutes, he told himself. On the day after Slotin vanished, another part of the future had shown itself to Leo. He was lying in the hospital bed, weary, full of grief and indecision. A deliberate, hearty knock, and before he said anything, General Groves had marched in and closed the door. Straight as a board in his uniform. In his hand was a piece of paper. Leo saw it, and looked up at Groves's face. Groves smiled, an insincere grin. He had the face of a man who knew what he wanted and would have it. Leo struggled to sit up, to appear to be at least one inch taller. Groves pulled a metal chair up beside the bed, squeaking it on the floor. He asked Leo pleasantly how he was feeling, and Leo replied that he was better, never taking his eyes off the paper.

"There is something we need to take care of," Groves said, smiling again. Leo nodded. Groves took the paper from his lap and placed it quietly on the bed. It lay on the spread, white on white.

"I'll leave this with you," Groves said. "We look forward to your return to work." He stood up.

"Yes," Leo replied.

It was brief. He would agree that Slotin had committed suicide, a rash young man. Unfortunate. A simple calculation: a signature in exchange for his future on the Project.

All of what had been underneath his thoughts as he calculated and poured energy into solving each piece of the puzzle as it came before him, as he took the pill each night that sent him into sleep, came slowly up, as if seeping up through layers of stone and clay. He saw, even as the scientists had thought they were the smart ones, who had been in charge all along. What came to his mind was simple. Los Alamos was not a lab, it was a factory. The people who owned the bomb will own the world.

In the snow, Leo touched the letter in his pocket again. He worked on the wording: "Please exercise your power as commander in chief to rule that, in the present phase of the war, the United States shall not drop the atomic bomb on Japan."

He looked up and saw, at the edge of the horizon, what looked like a box. Hope started up in his chest even as he tried to tamp it down. He began walking with some speed, ignoring the pain in his ankle and the raw feel of the cold in his lungs. His legs were leaden, as if filled with something heavier than blood and flesh. It was a house that was little more than a mud hut, with a broken tractor and a scrawny dog lying under the *portal*. A string of red chile laced with snow hung beside the blue door. The dog stood up and its hackles rose. It began to skirt its way toward him, growling. Leo flapped his arms against his body in the thin jacket. He worked his way along the side of the road farthest from the dog. He saw a little collection of adobes. Then, a round shape that was a gas pump and a small structure that might have been a store. As the dog circled nearer, Leo ran around the pump, through a layer of mud, and up the two steps to the porch of the store. The dog barked, but stood still. Leo peered through the window. A man was standing in front of a row of shelves that held boxes of Kellogg's Corn Flakes, resting his hand on a glass case full of candles. Leo pulled at the door, which creaked and resisted. Inside, he felt a bit of warmth. The man looked at him without speaking.

Leo stood in front of him, shivering. Finally, he said through chattering teeth, "I am lost."

The man replied, *"No hablo inglés,"* and smiled.

"La Posada?" Leo said stupidly. He flapped his arms. The man walked around from the back of the counter and took his arm. As he leaned on the man's arm, Leo felt the room spin and tip. The cornflakes formed one large rooster of red and white and yellow. He tried to grab at the case in front of him as he went down.

2

Milagros

TEN

Eleanor stood at the window, picking dried flowers off the geranium plants in the last of the evening light. The snow had melted almost entirely, except under the pinions, where it lay like white skirts thrown down on the damp earth. Everything was still. The black mesa to the west seemed more deeply fixed in the earth, and the trees on the hills nearby were motionless, stiff with cold. Her garden looked as if a great hand had passed over it, quelling its growth. She felt she had entered a play in which the actors had all been ceaselessly moving and were now suddenly frozen in place.

She held the dry perfumed husks in her hands, as if establishing their weight. How to weigh something so weightless? "What would you save first from a burning building?" she and her friends had asked each other at art school. "A Picasso or a puppy?" What would be the weight of a sister's love for a brother, or a brother's for a sister, or, for that matter, a husband's for a wife? How would you choose? Or the weight of the future, of possibility, against the present. She thought of Jesus tunneling back from the dead, a gossamer figure, thin as lace, threading his way through keyholes in locked doors. To say over and over, Take this second chance. Begin again.

She had taken Walker Stern's money from Betsy and then, realizing she could not open a bank account without her husband's co-signature, given it back.

"Keep this for me, Bets," she said. "Just for now." Betsy solemnly took the check and placed it back in her green suede purse.

On the way home, Eleanor bought a tin of smoked tongue, Edgar's favorite, and stopped at the liquor store for a bottle of chilled champagne.

When she opened the door, carrying her packages, Edgar was already there, washing his hands.

She placed the packages on the table and unwrapped them. Edgar, seeing the champagne, smiled and said, "Well, whatever are we celebrating?" He took it from her hands.

She decided the way to do it was just to dive in.

"I sold some paintings this morning," she said. "Betsy brought Walker Stern by the studio, and he bought three."

"What!" Edgar said, his face turning red. "You sold work without my permission!"

"Permission?" Eleanor asked, both frightened and angry. "I don't believe we wanted that word to be part of our marriage."

Edgar slammed down the bottle on the kitchen counter, and it cracked at the bottom, sending champagne spilling onto the floor.

"How dare you!" he yelled, bringing his fist close to her face. "How dare you sell work without telling me. I suppose you sold those lurid figures."

Eleanor fought shock. "Yes," she said, "and they brought quite a sum."

Edgar stood still for a moment, and then he whispered, "Your ambition knows no bounds. You want to wear the pants in this family," and then he walked out the door, slamming it behind him. Eleanor stood in the kitchen, holding her fists to her mouth, tears falling onto her hands.

The painting had stopped after that, and her headaches and fear of the streets had begun. Edgar was kind and dutiful. Then Betsy invited her to go out to New Mexico to see Mabel Dodge, and Edgar told her he thought it would be good for her. She remembered now, standing at her kitchen window with the geranium husks in her hands, how she had watched that landscape present itself after the long, flat plains: the Sangre de Cristos rising up, the high thin air, the desert's lavish light. Her heart had lifted to meet them. She and Betsy had enjoyed Mabel's hospitality and then returned to New York, as they said they would, after a month. Edgar had greeted them at the station with an armful of roses.

The next summer when she decided to return, alone this time, to Santa Fe, Edgar was not so pleased, but she promised him that she would come back, after six weeks. The day she left, she noticed he was limping slightly when he walked, and it took all her effort to keep her resolve and get out the door. Once in New Mexico, she finally found the courage to buy a few paints and to begin. She bought the land without telling him, with part of the money from the second Stern sale, and hired Esteban to begin to build the house. She told herself it was a summer place and she would persuade Edgar to join her there. The week she returned to New York, the headaches began again.

And then her father died. A week later, she packed her bags.

Edgar had walked into the room.

"And what, pray tell, are you doing?" he asked.

"I am returning to New Mexico," she said.

"I thought that was finished."

"Why did you think that?"

"A wife really cannot leave her husband for months on end and expect him to agree."

Guilt filled her lungs. "Edgar," she said, "I can't paint here anymore. I can hardly paint there, but I must try. You might come, too," she said softly, "if you chose?"

"We have spoken of that. You know I cannot travel. My lungs are much too weak to withstand foreign germs."

"Oh, Edgar," she said, putting her hand on his sleeve. "You are strong as an ox."

He pushed her hand away. "You belittle me."

"No," she said. "I only thought—"

"Be quiet," he said. "If you must gad about the country, go quickly." And he stalked out of the room.

She should stay, she thought. She should prune herself to fit him, but instead she picked up her bags, whispered promises through his shut door, and left the apartment. On the train, when she slept, dreams possessed her. Her ghost father tipping his hat. Edgar standing in the kitchen, a bottle of champagne breaking in his hands.

After Eleanor had been in Santa Fe for three weeks, she sent Edgar her post office address. He wrote back, "What has happened to the wife you were?"

Eleanor didn't know how to answer. She trembled when she heard the passage from Ezekiel read at church: "And I will give you a heart of flesh rather than a heart of stone." Mine must be made of marble, she thought, but she remained in New Mexico. Just for the summer, she told herself; she would return to him when the aspens turned from green to gold.

She bought the Ford from a man who had worked for the Bureau of Indian Affairs and wanted to go back home. Back to a place, he said, where you don't have to water the lawn. She took it down to get a ration sticker and drove it back to the hotel.

She practiced the words for *goodbye* and *good morning* by listening to the maids talking at the hotel. *Adios. Buenos dias.* The word for the strings of red chile that hung by the doors in the fall: *ristras.* The word *mesa* was not only a table but also a square straight-edged hill. This other culture, and its language, became a place she traveled to when the pressure on her heart was too great. *"Ande yo caliente ya riase la gente,"* Estaban had said, as he smoothed the plaster over her new fireplace. *As long as I am warm, let the people laugh.*

One evening she was invited to the home of a man who said he had heard of her from Mabel Dodge. He knew of her show in New York, the paintings and their price. His house was a spare adobe out at the end of Canyon Road. Eleanor opened the gate, made of many small weathered pieces of wood arranged in an intricate pattern, walked up a flagstone path, and knocked on the equally rustic door. Mr. Alexander opened it, a small man with a fringe of dark hair, wearing a pair of blue jeans with a silver concho belt, and boots. He ushered her in. Before her ran a long hallway lined in shallow shelves, from floor to ceiling. On them was what he called "folk art." He gestured to the shelves with an open, white hand. She was meant to linger, to admire. Kachina dolls. Tiny silver medallions in the shapes of arms and legs, an eye. "*Milagros,*" he said. "Meaning miracles. A charm against something bad, or a prayer, I suppose. Quaint, don't you think?

"And here," he said, "*retablos,* or religious paintings, thanks-givings for cures." Eleanor picked up St. Sebastian painted on a tobacco can.

A being carved from white bone with turquoise eyes, the length of her index finger. "A Zuni fetish," he said. "Very valuable." In the cor-ner, a child's chair with St. Guadalupe painted on the seat and "Señora, pray for us" written in Spanish on the back. Eleanor was suddenly sickened.

"Where did you get these?" she asked.

"I acquired them," he said.

Over dinner, he turned to her and said, as if out of the blue, "Is Mr. Stanton going to be joining you soon?"

She looked him in the eye. "Mr. Stanton only rarely travels," she said.

"That's convenient," the collector said. "Do you have—what shall I call it—an arrangement?"

"No," Eleanor replied, standing up from the table. "We do not."

.   .   .

She turned away from the window, crushed the dead petals in her palm. She thought of Leo, standing by the door as he had when she was getting ready to drive into town, his eyes on the keys in her hand. His look of surprise, and then—what? Acceptance. No, more like recognition. That she was just like all the rest. She felt the stillness she had been standing in shrink and evaporate, the way the sun licks away fog from a lake.

After Bill had left the night before, she had eaten her solitary dinner and gone to bed. She had woken up throughout the night, throwing pinion logs on the fire, trying to sort the thoughts in her mind. She should have been relieved, she felt, but she was more distressed than she had been in weeks.

In the morning, she had risen, washed her face, and pulled on her flannel bathrobe, the same one Leo had worn. As she was making coffee, she looked outside to see Griefa's wagon pulling up to the front gate.

She opened the door, letting in the chill air. Griefa climbed down and walked into the yard. Eleanor called out, "Good morning, Griefa."

"Good morning."

"I hadn't expected you today. Would you like some coffee?"

Griefa nodded. "I didn't finish yesterday."

Eleanor poured her a cup and then said, "I have a question for you: do you know where the man, Leo, went yesterday? When I got home he was gone."

"He left."

"While you were still here?"

"Yes."

"Do you know where he went?"

"No," Griefa said.

"He may have been a spy."

Griefa looked at her as if looking at a child. She shook her head.

Eleanor moved a step closer to her. "You don't think so."

"*Yo no se.*"

Eleanor, exasperated, said, "I should know. I've been keeping—I suppose I should say 'harboring'—him in my house for ten days."

Griefa looked down at the table, where she saw the remains of Eleanor's dinner, a strand of spaghetti stuck to the pale yellow plate and a bit of reddish sauce smudged on its lip. She picked up the plate and moved toward the sink. Then she turned and said, "Señora Eleanor, why do you ask me about him?"

"I ask because . . ." Eleanor hesitated. Why, indeed? "I don't know, Griefa."

She turned and walked back to the bedroom and sat down on the recently vacated bed. Griefa's question had caused a little chink to appear in the story she had told herself of what she had done the day before. Through that narrow opening, what flooded her was the memory of Leo's eyes on hers. More than memory—she felt physically back in the scene. His pale eyes, the color almost of turquoise stones, and her eyes rising to meet his. It was a greeting of two equals, she knew now; it had neither the anxiety nor the dread of her painful relations with Edgar. Her irritation and shyness with him were suddenly clear to her. Oh, how stupid, she thought. How did I not see it before? She sat on her bed and felt again her pleasure at *letting him in.* Then, what followed: Griefa's entrance into the room, the white paper on the desk, her stomach-dropping fear. But why, she thought today, why had she not simply asked him what the letter meant?

What happened then was like one of those newsreels in the theater shown before the film began: grainy, the people jerkily crossing space: she saw Edgar in her studio, standing in front of the figure painting. Edgar letting himself down into his armchair, his right hand clutching his linen handkerchief and his left reaching for her hand to pull her toward him. Then she understood what had driven her to go into town to ask for Bill's help. She jumped up, took a skirt and shirt from the *trastero*, pulled them on, and rushed past Griefa out the door, throwing an "I'll be right back" over her shoulder.

She had knocked on Bill's door and spoken to him all at once and turned away so as not to change her mind.

She had driven the road back slowly, fearing the body lying in a ditch. Nothing. Even as she searched for Leo, Edgar remained at the edge of her consciousness. She must write to him. Would he actually travel to see her? When she returned, Griefa had left; the house was clean.

As she stood now in her kitchen, she could feel in herself the seasons apart from Edgar, her daily prayers, her love of the desert, the companionship of Bill and Estaban and Griefa and not to forget Rita, adding up; they had *accumulated*. She held the sum of them.

She walked over to the edge of her living room and turned a canvas so that it faced her.

ELEVEN

L a Posada was the hotel in town where men checked in on the nights their wives threw them out. A collection of little adobes (some of which had frightening, badly wired kitchenettes) built "pueblo-style" around a winding narrow driveway. The hotel's ancient swimming pool, yet to be filled for the season, had a scummy puddle at the bottom, near which sat a quiet toad.

Spring had returned to Santa Fe, the sudden snow forgotten. The lilacs lining the twisting roads of the city were leafing out, and the green points of daffodil and crocus bulbs were pushing up through heavy wet clay. Leo sat on the narrow bed in his room, smoking, contemplating the red brick floor. Brick, Leo thought. Why do they make the floors out of what civilized people use for walls? The room was dingy, dusty. It held the bed, a rough table near the window, and a round-backed chair made of leather stretched over a willow wood frame, which made a noise like a bleating goat when he sat down in it. Fraying curtains in a calico print hung from the windows, which opened or refused to open with a rusty iron pull that Leo feared would break if he used it once too often. The screen had a hole in it through which newly hatched wasps regularly traveled.

After the man from the store had practically carried him into the hotel, Leo had slept for a good twelve hours. Awaking hungry and rested, he ordered room service and sat down to what they called here an enchilada with pinto beans and rice. Peasant food, not his favorite. He had finished the letter, sealed it, and, having received directions from a clerk, walked carefully to the nearby post office, slipped the letter into the slot with the brass lettering, and left, only looking up to see the calendar on the wall, one of those with just the date. April 3.

After that, he simply waited. He kept himself to his room or the tiny walled patio in front of it. There had always been rumors on the Hill of the men who stood around the plaza, the only ones who wore suits and ties in this country of the bolo tie and the blue jean. Leo, who had left Berlin on a train on April Fool's Day 1933, two months and a day after Hitler was appointed chancellor, who knew that the whole trick of existence is not necessarily to be much cleverer than other people but just to be one day earlier, could not quite figure out what was true here and what was what he called, to himself and once to Slotin, Jewish paranoia. (Slotin had replied that no Jew was paranoid; no psyche, he said, was capable of manufacturing what the world had dished out to Jews.)

He was scrupulous in keeping his mind off Eleanor Garrigue. When he slipped, usually on waking in the early hours of the cold mornings, when a whisper of her wrist traced its way through his cells, he threw it back into the recesses, only to have another image of her rise, if not the next morning, then the next. God knows who she went to, keys in hand, cold determination on her face. To whom had she betrayed him? This question daily intruded.

He forced his thoughts away from her by doing push-ups on the hard floor. How had he wound up here? He went back to the start. He had planned to be an engineer. In the aftermath of the first war, Czechoslovakia threw off the Austro-Hungarian Empire and became a democracy under Masaryk. Some light fell on his people in that brief time. Leo remembered the case of the Jewish man accused of a ritual killing of a Christian child and Charlotte Garrigue Masaryk's fierce defense of him. Leo's father, a prosperous druggist, sent him to Charles University. From there, he had applied for a visa to Germany and made his way to Berlin. Lotte was headed for chemistry at Charles. Both of their parents died within a year of each other, leaving their young adult children alone to face the rest of the twentieth century.

Berlin was being rebuilt before Leo's eyes: the old aristocracy had withdrawn, leaving a society of journalists, intellectuals, artists, and actors. Mies van der Rohe was erecting a new building of glass. The currency was falling, requiring that one buy one's food early in the week, before it rose in price. Leo bought eggs not to cook but to trade for theater tickets. He fell asleep in the engineering lectures, and finally someone told him to go to the University of Berlin and talk to Professor Einstein. "What do you want?" Einstein had asked.

Leo had taken to the world of atoms and thermodynamics, pollen floating in water, heat. He solved problems by walking in the gray snowy streets, past a woman without legs, plunked down in front of a bank, who sold, ironically, shoelaces. He had wasted so much time in engineering that after a year he asked for a thesis problem. Probably to test him, his professor, not Einstein, gave him what Leo later thought was an unsolvable problem in relativity theory. He worked on it for six months, and then the Christmas holiday came and he thought Christmas was not for working but for loafing, so he loafed by walking around the city. Past the torso who sold shoelaces, van der Rohe's glass castle, the bars and cabarets. What came into his mind was a paradox in thermodynamics. He walked, and sat down in the evenings and wrote it all down. By the end of the Christmas holiday, he felt he had it. Tentative, afraid to address his professor, he took it to Einstein, who told him when he presented his idea that it was impossible and after ten minutes said, "I like this very much."

He was Dr. Kavan by the end of May.

.   .   .

In the middle of the next week, a knock on the door. The boy handed him a thin yellow envelope.

He had opened it so carefully, it might have been made of glass. "I have given your letter to T, who promises to place it on R's desk," Judge Frankfurter wrote. "R is presently sitting for his portrait at Warm Springs. Fond regards, F." Leo felt a flow of relief, and sat down. That evening, he dined on chicken stew with small chunks of potatoes and carrots. He sat at the little desk afterward, sipping a whiskey. He felt some part of his strength returning. Using what little information he had, he calculated his odds: His distance from the collision of the hemispheres. The length of time spent in the blue-lit, radiation-filled room. The three men, three points, a triangle. A point, Euclid said, is that which has no part. Two points make a line. He thought of Frisch's cat, clumps of its fur left lying on the blanket as it staggered across the floor. He wondered how the student was faring and, as if in an experiment, what his blood was doing, inside his veins, hidden from view. And the cells in his bone marrow. He thought of his father's copy of da Vinci's dissection notes: one had to get over the fear of being in a room in the night with a body, gruesomely exposed, da Vinci noted. Yet, remarkable how little blood there was, except for the capillaries. How complex was the beauty of the body. When da Vinci moved to Paris, on his shopping list was a human skull. His habit was to buy wild birds in the market to draw their wings, then carry them to the hills to open the doors of the cage and watch them fly away.

You who kill a man, da Vinci said, think on this. You murder all that is in a man. You kill his body, all the beauty of its workings; but worse even than destroying his heart, which gives life to the brain, you murder that thing inside him, the center of all that is this man and no other.

It was da Vinci, Leo had learned later, who invented the submarine, drawing intricate tubes with periscopes and breathing apparatus, but he destroyed his models when he realized they could be used to build dangerous instruments of war.

Even as he speculated on it, Leo felt his health improving. Perhaps he had been just far enough away from the collision of the spheres to make it, as Slotin had thought he would. He told himself that what was important now was to wait, to see if his letter would have any effect at all on the history of the world. The Germans were in full retreat. The war would be over soon. If Lotte was alive—at this thought he sighed, and stood and walked to the tiny window. If she was alive, he would be what she had left. And she would be all he had of his family.

He walked back to the bed and sat down. Once he got an answer, he would leave this strange desert exile, return to the Met Lab, and rally his old colleagues in Chicago. They could organize a demonstration of the bomb before representatives from the UN, in a desert or on a barren island. "You see what sort of a weapon we had but did not use."

And after? He had not even thought about an "after that." Now, as he sat in the little room with the ugly, uncomfortable floors and wasps for company, he considered his future. Would it be possible to return to the search for what was true? To comprehend the world's secret, invisible workings, beauty he had once sought by inquiry, by imagination, and by experiment. His own religion. And what had been released out of that box when he understood the splitting of neutrons would be placed back inside. Or put to good use. What a frail hope, he thought. Then, despite himself, Leo remembered Eleanor talking, her face lit with intelligence, about Jesus and Satan. He wondered if she actually believed in the devil or the business of Jesus being God, so costly, to put it mildly, to his people. Yet the metaphor of stones into bread was a perfect one; a magical solution, requiring only a fundamental transformation of molecules. He wondered if Satan, too, was bent on practicality.

"Bah," he said to himself. The image of her face and her eyes holding his made him ache. How had he managed to let that happen!

His eyes closed and his mind drifted to Slotin walking gallantly out of the lab, and then to Lotte playing hopscotch in front of their house in Prague, leaning over in that city's gold light to pick up a stone.

TWELVE

Fermi walked up the canyon carrying the guillotine rods, with David and Kistiakowsky beside him.

"I'm going to call this canyon Omega," Fermi said. "Or maybe we should call it Otto."

Otto Frisch had kept up his feverish work on the uranium hydride assemblies. He had stacked and restacked the uranium hydride bars with their international provenance: mined in the Congo, moved by railroad to Middlesex, New Jersey, and Tonowanda, New York, to a Union Carbide plant, refined, then shipped in small heavy boxes to Oak Ridge for inspection, and finally shipped by train or car to Los Alamos. Two suitcases weighing ten pounds each were carried by courier in the back seat of a Chevrolet sedan. Forty pounds were shipped by train from Knoxville to Chicago to Los Angeles on the Super Chief, and finally to the "Calexico Engineering Company," in Albuquerque, where they were diverted to a railroad siding on the outskirts of the city and then driven to Los Alamos by "Smith," who went to Albuquerque once a month for a cello lesson. One by one, Otto built cubes, like children's log cabins. Around them, to save on the amount of uranium he would have to use, he built frameworks of beryllium bricks that would reflect neutrons into the pile. He built dozens and dozens of assemblies for faster and faster reactions to measure just how much energy was released, exactly what it took, how much uranium, how large an assembly. But he could not allow

the pile to go critical. Or everything—the child's log cabin of uranium bars, the men who stood next to it, the suddenly built city of
Los Alamos—all this would end in fire. He had seen it up close, with
Lady Godiva, the red lamps glowing red, and he did not want to see
it again.

But it was not enough to build assemblies that were almost critical,
because you could not know exactly what it would take, finally, to
make this particular gadget work. Frisch wore a path around the
pond outside G lab that cold winter of 1944–45, kicking at the stones
that poked out of the snowdrifts, pondering this problem. One evening, in the waning winter light that filled the sky with red streaks and
colored the mountains, he remembered a bakery of his youth in
Vienna. The baker in his long white apron stood in the early morning
light, punching out the hole in the middle of a doughnut. What if,
Frisch thought that night, as he stopped at the edge of the frozen
pond, you had an assembly that was critical only for an instant—as
Lady Godiva had been the evening he leaned in too close—then sub-
critical again. What if he made an assembly with a hole in the middle
that would allow neutrons to escape so that no chain reaction could
begin? But the missing part, the missing doughnut piece, was constructed in such a way as to be dropped through the hole, passing
through it in a split second. For that moment, there would be the
condition for an atomic explosion, and then it would pass. It would
be the condition of an explosion, Frisch thought, *but only barely so.*

"Tickling the dragon's tail," Slotin, laughing, remarked that night
over dinner in the mess hall. "Mighty big dragon."

Frisch took a bite of his dinner and turned to Leo Kavan.

"It's crazy," he said, "but is it really crazy enough?"

By April 1945, Oak Ridge had produced enough U-235 to allow a
near-critical assembly of pure metal. Frisch received the boxes of the
bars of uranium and set them well apart from each other in his lab.

First they were silver, and then, exposed to the oxygen in the air, they turned a watery blue and then a deep rich purple, like summer plums. Fermi designed and began to build the contraption he affectionately called the guillotine.

While Frisch worked at the science of a near explosion, the invasion of Europe moved apace. David read much of the news in the papers, but other pieces came from the rumors that floated through the Project like the seeds from cottonwoods. General Groves had assembled a strike force to travel with the front lines to find what might be the German atomic bomb factories, and the 1,200 tons of uranium the Germans had confiscated when they invaded Belgium in 1940. The men drove into Paris, taking sniper fire, and snaked through the country, following trails of evidence found in labs. Groves would not rest, he said, until they accounted for every pound.

In Toulouse, they found thirty-one tons. These were sent back to the United States by steamer, processed through Oak Ridge, and sent to Los Alamos.

In Stassfurt, Germany, near Magdeburg, near the place where the misericords lay under the monks' haunches, they found a looted and bombed plant where piles of papers were stacked and scattered. The ore was stored aboveground in barrels, some broken. There were 1,100 tons.

And on a cliff in Haigerloch, Germany, they found the rest, Frisch told Fermi one night as they walked away from the Tech Area. It was in a cave behind a steel door, a concrete pit. In it were two thick metal cylinders, one within the other, covered by a heavy metal shield. Inside the inner vessel were one and a half tons of heavy water and more than six hundred bricks of metallic uranium hanging from chains in the water. This was what was left of the German atomic machine.

David lay on his back on his bed and thought about what would happen now. The Germans were finished, yes? But nothing seemed to be slowing down. When Oppenheimer and Ken Bainbridge had left the Hill last fall for a protracted amount of time, with sleeping bags and a weapons carrier, had they found a spot to test the gadget?

In Omega Canyon, Fermi built a ten-foot iron frame to support two aluminum poles. He surrounded the frame with beryllium bricks to the height of a table. He would raise a uranium hydride slug to the top. Like the blade of a guillotine, it would fall, and as it passed between the blocks it would momentarily form, Frisch hoped, a critical mass.

Arcs of snow still lay on the northern slopes. Frisch carried the uranium slug, the size of a chocolate bar, in a box up the slope. As he hiked into the canyon, his thoughts strayed from the experiment ahead of him to Leo Kavan. Kavan had left a note on Frisch's desk, how many weeks ago? Saying he was going on a leave, to recover, to grieve his friend. Frisch knew all too well what had happened to Slotin, that risk taker who grew to love the dragon and its tail. Could it have been a month ago? I should have done more for him, Frisch thought. Ahead of him, he saw through the trees the guillotine and put thoughts of Leo Kavan aside.

He and Fermi stood, hands in their pockets, looking at the poles gleaming in the early sun. Then they went to work.

The slug was lifted into place, and Frisch held up his hand and then dropped it, like a flagman at a car race. The slug fell through space, an igniter of worlds, to the bricks below. The monitors registered a burst of neutrons and a temperature rise, in just that split second.

"Everything happened exactly as it should," Frisch said to Fermi, cuffing him on the shoulder. "A critical mass, *but only barely so.* Just like a stifled explosion."

"We are there," Fermi replied. "It is only a matter of mechanics now."

Frisch would deliver to Oppenheimer that night the first and actual "determination of the critical mass of pure U-235."

David Stein felt the intensity gathering as he watched the guillotine experiment succeed.

As they hiked down together from Omega Canyon, Frisch was laughing, and the men around him tripped over one another to be the one nearest to him. David walked alone.

THIRTEEN

Griefa worked beside Eleanor, spring cleaning, as Eleanor called it. Griefa admired Eleanor's cooking, but not her housekeeping. In the early days, Griefa had watched Eleanor dust by flinging a feathered thing around as if holding a chicken by its neck. Griefa pointed out gently that such a duster might be useful somewhere where dirt did not penetrate everywhere, did not come in through the windows and creep up under the plaster on the walls and blow from the west every spring, removing, as Estaban said, all of the dirt from the Grand Canyon in Arizona and placing it here in New Mexico. Somewhere, Griefa thought but did not say, where the houses were not made of dirt.

Today, they were turning the bed and couch mattresses, washing the sheets and hanging them outside, and airing the blankets. Griefa cleaned behind the stove, collected the dust mixed with grease into the cloth, and crushed a black widow spider under her heel. She noticed with pleasure that the floor was still without cracks after two years, and deep bloodred from the steer killed on it, whose blood the dancers had pushed into the soil with their feet, mixing and dancing, a long pattern of feet over many hours. Eleanor had run from the house when she realized how the floor was to be made, and the dancers had looked at her with surprise. Where did she think you got that color red? Griefa had let the floor dry and had then polished it to the specifications of the lead singer from the pueblo, with Johnson's floor wax and two friends who worked with rags wrapped around their hands and knees.

Eleanor was working in the bedroom with a mad energy, as if all of her body had to be used up. She was sleeping in her own bed again.

Griefa had read Eleanor's letters from her husband and the few records Eleanor kept about herself. Breaches of privacy Griefa looked on as her obligation as a servant to keep one step ahead of one's boss, even if one's boss was seemingly decent, like Eleanor. A boss was a boss. She had read all of Teddy's letters, including the endless recipes. She prayed for him when she prayed, which was not very often, as she was experiencing a loss of faith. Her priest was a boring young man, and the priests had stifled the nuns at her grade school, the only educated people she had known. She knew from her own life that sex was pleasing, that too many children rendered a woman powerless, and that the pope lived in a palace a long way from New Mexico.

Until last fall, Griefa had lived in the small village of Polvadera, in the south of New Mexico, a tiny village square surrounded by wide fields of alfalfa along the Rio Grande. She had loved to drive her cart to nearby Monticello, where there was an adobe church on the square with a white bell tower; inside tapered candles in a wrought-iron stand made by a blacksmith in Magdalena burned in the dusty light. She walked along the irrigation ditches that opened with a wood gate that made a sucking sound as it left the mud, controlled by the local *majordomo,* the ditch boss, who regulated the flow from the *acequia madre,* the mother ditch, depending on the snowpack and the rare rains. Water for drinking in those villages came from the ditches, the river, and one shallow well. So many people died of malaria. Typhoid took the life of a neighbor's older boy. Reading material was the Montgomery Ward catalog. Two automobiles were owned and sometimes driven in Monticello, a Model T Ford and a 1927 Chevrolet. Men from the villages left them to work every year in the silver mines in Colorado. In Water Canyon, near Monticello, snow often lay under aspen trees that were leafing out in curls of pale green.

Just south of these villages, west of the river, Griefa knew there was a place you did not go alone: a great parched landscape, stretching out under the sun like the backbone of a snake, miles of black rocks strewn with yucca and scorpions. Gray mountains at its edge scraped the sky. When Agustin Rodriguez, his fellow Franciscans, his sheep and goats, and a detachment of soldiers had marched through the mesquite in 1581, he had cursed it with this name: Jornada del Muerto, the journey of death.

One evening last fall, just before she moved to be close to her grandfather near Santa Fe, she was driving her cart along the main road that ran from northern New Mexico to the south. She was heading toward Monticello from Polvadera. She was singing to herself, and watching the red-winged blackbirds rise up from the fields. She heard a noise behind her and turned just in time to see a huge truck bearing down on her. Not a truck, she realized as she craned her neck and tried to calm her spooked horse. More like a war tank. A man with a submachine gun sat on its top. As they passed her, he gave Griefa a swift, dismissing glare.

Griefa liked to listen to Eleanor's radio as she cleaned. At La Posada where she also worked, the woman in charge of the maids was a *bruja*. Griefa thought she might be *loco en la cabeza*. Today, after working with Eleanor, she would have to go to the afternoon shift at the hotel, and then home to care for Estaban's younger son, who was slow. She hoped that after that, after all of the work, she might be able to sit for a few minutes by herself and think about the stories she heard that day. Or what things occurred to her while she heard them, or how she might mix them together into another story.

Griefa listened to the radio that afternoon, as she did every time she was at Eleanor's house, and made sure she remembered what was said so she could tell her mother. Her mother could not see and could not afford a radio. When things were bad in Griefa's life, her mother said to her, "It is the meal given you."

Today she was listening to Fibber McGee and Molly. Mr. Wilcox was talking about gas rationing and the need to save the rubber on tires. McGee said he thought the government should have foreseen the problem and done something about it. Griefa privately agreed.

"Well, everybody can't be as farsighted as you are, dearie," Molly says.

"Is he pretty farsighted, Molly?"

"Why, he's uncanny, Mr. Wilcox. He's the one who said we'd lick the Japanese in ten days. Remember?"

Griefa removed the geraniums from the sill and cleaned the dirt from underneath them, cupping her palm to catch it. She walked to the door and tossed the dirt out into what Eleanor called her garden and what Griefa called the dirt in the front of the house. She turned back to the room to survey her work.

"Though I will say he made one accurate prediction."

"And what was that?"

"Well, last night he said, 'Well, tomorrow is another day.' And sure enough, it was."

Griefa considered what she had seen at the hotel yesterday. As she walked along the little road connecting the adobes, she saw a man dressed in a suit, leaning against the *hoven* outside the dining room, smoking. He had been around, buying Juicy Fruit gum in the gift shop, salting his eggs in the dining room, picking up an *Albuquerque Journal,* every day something new, for several days. It was sometimes helpful to be invisible. The man who used an excess of salt did not see her. She remembered clearly the first time she became invisible, as if a magic cloak were thrown over her. She was cleaning a toilet in the house of the woman who lived on Canyon Road, a "collector" from Texas. (Ah, New Mexico, her father had said, so far from heaven, so close to Texas.) She was sixteen. Griefa was on her hands and knees, removing the stains from the shit of the collector, when the woman came into the bathroom, washed her hands, and then walked out again. She had been standing two inches from Griefa's right hand, a foot from Griefa's right knee. She had said nothing to her. She was talking to a friend in the other room; her voice never faltered.

"She said that tulips often die so beautifully—isn't that quaint?"

Griefa had finished cleaning the toilet, stood up, and washed her hands at the same sink. She had thought nothing. No thought had entered her head. As she left, she reached into the medicine cabinet and removed a single bottle of aspirin, placing it carefully in the pocket of her dress. Since that time, she had stolen small items from each of her employers, exacting a fee for their unconscious entitlement. At home, she has a tube of yellow paint belonging to Eleanor. She asked her grandfather once, a medicine man from San Ildefonso pueblo, why the Anglos were so capable of so many things and what she should do about it. Observe them, he replied.

Eleanor refilled a bowl of water that sat on the windowsill of the bedroom; Griefa had taught her to put some tiny amount of humidity into the air so her nose did not start, unaccountably, to bleed. She pulled off the sheets from her bed and washed them, then gathered the wet weight into her arms—her shirt was blotched with a wet stain—and carried it outside. She hung the sheets on the line—two white tents—and stood back. She might paint sheets on a line someday, floating white squares against a blue sky. When the sheets were dry, Eleanor picked them off the line and inhaled their sunny smell. Dark clouds were forming over the Sangres to the east. Eleanor carried the sheets inside and remade the bed.

He was gone without a trace, as water closes over a stone. She was alone again. Rather than the contentment she had felt in her house, she felt as lonely as the first night he had stayed with her. She stood in the bedroom on the woven rug she bought from the women in Los Ojos, in the north, who worked together at large looms in an old store with a high tin roof and told ribald jokes over cups of coffee. She thought she might drive up there to paint if she could save the gas. No word from Teddy. In the first months he had been held in the camp; after the initial postcard from the Red Cross, she had sometimes received packets of letters with different dates, shipped all at once. But now, for a month, nothing. And she had not managed to complete a letter to Edgar. How to duck him, keep him mollified? She had once wished that he would come to New Mexico, but now when she envisioned him walking through the door, she felt sick at heart.

From the bedroom, she heard an announcer's voice instead of Fibber McGee and Molly. Eleanor walked into the living room just as Griefa turned the volume knob to the right. "We interrupt this broadcast," the man was saying. And then Eleanor brought her hands to her face.

The president was sitting for his portrait at Warm Springs when he complained of a headache.

In the late afternoon, Leo heard a tap at his door. When he opened it, he saw Jesus, the man who delivered firewood, tears washing his cheeks.

"*El presidente,*" he said, holding out his hands to Leo.

"What?" Leo said, taking the man's gnarled fingers in his. "What are you saying?"

"*El presidente,*" Jesus said again, and wept. "He is died."

"No," Leo said. "President Roosevelt? The president?"

Jesus nodded, wiping his face.

Leo turned away, pushed his hair back from his forehead. His letter. What was the fate of his letter? Jesus pulled at him.

"*La radio,*" Jesus said. And Leo followed him out the courtyard of his adobe to the kitchen, where the cook and the waitresses and waiters were standing around an old Victrola in a silence so concentrated, Leo knew that what Jesus had said was true. The body would be brought back to Washington by train. Truman had been sworn in. A man chewing gum stood outside, reading the newspaper, as if oblivious to the changing fortunes of nations.

Leo's letter lay on the president's desk, he later learned, unopened, unread.

FOURTEEN

Bill rose early on Sunday to prepare for the service, and to reread his sermon on Roosevelt's death. It had snowed again last night, another spring storm, and Bill looked out into the yard and saw white marshmallow-like mounds that the day before had been spring lilacs. The snow-cushioned silence was consoling. The loss of Roosevelt had stunned him into grief. He felt closer to Jesus, in his low state, in his affliction with those who suffer. His first thought on waking was of Roosevelt, then of Eleanor Garrigue, then of David—his own Trinity.

He hadn't seen Eleanor since her sudden arrival at his door. She had missed church last Sunday. He had not worked out how to tell her he had spoken to David. Nervousness lingered at the edge of his consciousness, a nagging doubt. Don't fret about it, he told himself. It was important for me to protect her. That's my job as her priest. She may have gotten into something bigger than she imagined— something I still don't understand.

Bill sighed. He put on his clerical shirt and lifted his collar from the top of the bureau. He picked up the gold stud from a bowl and, holding it in one hand, placed the collar around his neck, then reached back and secured it with the stud. He looked at the man in the mirror. Brown eyes, a bit of gray at the temples. A neat face, handsome to some.

What really was the job of a priest, he thought, as he made himself a pot of coffee, and poured cream into a pitcher his parishioners had given him when they discovered he liked café au lait. (How they noticed his every habit, his slightest inclination.) In the refrigerator was another casserole someone had dropped off last night, shoved into the icebox without his knowing it, this one a canned salmon surprise, the tiny round eye-socket bones still present, as he had unhappily discovered. On Easter afternoon, he had baptized a baby who looked up at him with quiet concentration as he had held her warm head in his cupped palm and dipped his other hand in the water three times. Father, Son, Holy Ghost. She blinked when the water splashed on her forehead but did not cry. He held the soft linen at the ready, and dried her hair quickly, as the day was cool. In that moment, he had thought how much he loved being a priest. As he held the baby, having made the eternal motion with his hand, he felt part of something that went back centuries, and more than that: the gift of a child, the gift of water, and our faithful acknowledgment of them.

He had wanted to be a minister for a very long time, keeping the news from his father while studying law until he told him by failing the bar exam twice. Late to the practice of it, his vocation was all the more dear. Yet it remained a mystery to him exactly what it was. Sometimes when he lifted the communion wafer up over the chalice of wine to break it in two, he allowed himself to lift up with it. If he managed to ignore the spiderweb hanging from one of the beams in the nave, and Mrs. Stanley's cough (she always signaled her impatience at this exact time; Mrs. Stanley found the celebration of Holy Communion "too papist"), his gaze traveled up to the frail circle of what his father called fish food and he sometimes almost saw the wafer changing, as if in a gentle twirl of light, into the openhearted body of Christ. There were Sundays when he felt as if a year passed between the raising up of the wafer and the fraction.

Open our hearts, Lord.

And our mouth shall proclaim Thy praise.

When he gives the Body to them, the gathered guests at this feast of longing, he looks into their upturned faces. A few allow their yearning to be seen; most do not. Their hands open to receive the wafers, and close again, like their hearts. People need so much. He wishes he could unlock them, just for a moment, so they could allow the world in, and all they are meant to receive, while putting down the burdens they are meant to relinquish.

He finished dressing and took up his sermon, hoping it had improved overnight. Doing justice to Roosevelt and easing the people's fear at losing a president during war felt much beyond him. Will I see Eleanor today? he wondered. Will I see her attentive face among those coughing or sleeping? Her direct, even gaze. Will she hear the phrases I turned just for her? Oh, Lord, he prayed, I know you can't make her love me, but let her notice my remarkable preaching.

FIFTEEN

After Roosevelt's death, Leo lay in his room, staring at the ceiling or barely unconscious in a fitful sleep. He was reduced to this, after his best connection to power was undone in the seconds it took for a brain to hemorrhage.

In the morning, he knew he must decide. He had to rework his strategy. He wrote a letter, sealed it, and walked out into the open. He was on his way back from the post office when he saw the man in the suit lounging beside the news rack in the lobby. Minutes later, as he walked quickly to his room, hoping to appear as casual as any tourist, he came upon the woman from Eleanor's house, the maid, her odd tall figure bent over a broom, sweeping outside his door. He motioned to her to move closer.

"Mrs. . . . ah . . . ?"

"*Sí?*" she said.

"You might remember me?"

"*Sí,*" she replied, and took up her broom again.

He told her of his thoughts.

"Señor Leo," she said loudly. He brushed his finger to his lips. "How far do you think my horse can walk? To Lamy? To the train? *Loco,*" she said under her breath. "Why don't you just hire a taxi?"

"Too public," he replied, and he glanced over his shoulder at the figure by the lobby doors.

"And even if I could borrow my brother's truck," Griefa said, "the gas would cost." She peered at him with a sly smile. He drew her toward his door.

"Can you at least get me out of this hotel?"

She considered, and then nodded.

"Tonight," she said.

Leo thanked her. She turned back to her broom.

At ten that night, Leo closed the door behind him and waited until his eyes adjusted to the dark. His knees felt flimsy. He turned to survey the courtyard. Nothing stirred. He bent down beside the plastered wall and shuffled along until he was behind his room; then he threw himself up on it as if mounting a bareback horse, scraping his hands on the rough plaster. He landed on the street, wiped his hands, and trotted across it to the grounds of St. Vincent's Hospital, where he sat down, hidden from the street by a cottonwood tree. The ravens that frequented this lawn were asleep. By his watch, she was late.

A truck appeared around the corner, rattling and grinding its gears; a dog on a nearby street began to bark and alerted all the mongrels in the neighborhood. Griefa slowed near where Leo was sitting and settled to a stop. He grimaced as he stood up; if anyone was following him certainly he would know just precisely where he was by now. He looked over his shoulder and hopped up onto the running board and into the passenger seat. Griefa did not look at him but motioned for him to move onto the floor, which he did, with some muttering about theatrics.

The truck coughed to a start and rumbled down the street as Leo hunched on the floor; the floorboards had holes in places, and he could see the street rushing by under his hands.

Griefa turned a corner and hit a bump in the road; Leo lurched, his head hit the glove box, and a beer can rolled out. "*Scheisse,*" he said.

They drove together, Griefa bent over the wheel, muttering, and

Leo cursing. Then the truck lurched to a stop. He smelled sage all around him, and smoke. Griefa opened the door, hopped out, and slammed the door shut. Leo climbed onto the seat and took his bearings. In front of him was the low shape of a dirt building, with a bench built into its side. A man was sitting on the bench with a blanket wrapped around him; neat white braids lay flat on his chest. He looked up at Leo briefly, as Griefa stooped to speak into his ear. He nodded, returned his glance to Leo, then stood up, gathered the blanket around him, and walked into the building. The dark closed behind him. Griefa opened the door to the truck and motioned for Leo to step down; he tried to shake off her hand on his arm as he hopped down. She pressed his arm more firmly and guided him into the doorway through which the old man had gone, and released him only once they were inside.

Smells came to him, the bodies of Indians, a sharp, sweet smell. The room was dark and small, a table, a chair, coals in a fireplace like the one Eleanor had in the corner of her living room, a cone of adobe darkened by soot. Griefa gestured to a blanket rolled on the floor near the fireplace and Leo, gratefully, sat down. She moved to another part of the room and returned with a piece of thick, greasy bread wrapped around some kind of smelly meat. Sheep, Leo thought as he took a bite and gagged.

Griefa walked out the door, and Leo lay down on the blanket and finally fell asleep. In the night he woke just enough to feel a wing of air as someone threw another blanket over him.

In the morning, he opened his eyes to see the man with the braids sitting by the fireplace, stoking the coals. Leo watched him, and as he did the man turned and looked at him, grave and opaque. Leo struggled to sit up. Outside he could hear people gathering. Talk. Griefa walked through the door, ignored Leo, and bent down to the man to whisper in his ear. He listened, then placed his hands on his knees and, grunting with old age, stood up. He walked with Griefa to the door and stood in the light. Leo got up and went looking for a bathroom. Griefa pointed to the door. As Leo climbed out, he found a small crowd of people outside who looked at him with some surprise and then returned to talking to the old man. Something is up, Leo thought, and I don't think it's me.

When Leo returned to the building, Griefa and the old man were inside again, sitting at the small table, covered by a plastic cloth with a pattern of pineapples on it, holding small bundles of sage wrapped in yarn in their hands. They were drinking from two shocking-pink pottery mugs.

"From Montgomery Ward," the old man said to Leo proudly, handing him a mug of coffee. He motioned for Leo to sit down with them, and when Leo sat, he said, "Good morning. How did you sleep?" Leo, surprised by the man's courtesy and fluency, replied, "Very well, thank you." And then he stopped for a minute. He put out his hand. "Leo Simms," he said. Griefa looked at him and frowned. The man nodded and said nothing.

She said, "My grandfather."

The man bundled the sage for a few minutes, and then turned to Leo and said softly, "The Corn Dance is held every year at this time. Our young men have been training in the kivas." He looked at the bundle in his hands. Leo began to speak, but the man again held up his hand. "But they have been told they must work." He gestured toward the door. "Up there."

Leo waited. He was trying to think.

"Up there," the man said again, and rested his hands on the table. " 'Extra shifts,' they call it."

"Ah," Leo said.

The old man was silent.

"May I ask you," Leo said, "where you went to school?"

The old man allowed a smile. A gold tooth. "In Boston," he replied. "A white woman sent me there. I lived with the Bullitt family in Watertown. The house had floors made of slate. It took a while for me to come home. Have you been to Boston?"

"No," Leo replied.

"It has a lot of red brick buildings," the old man replied.

Leo took a sip of the coffee. He held the cup, warming his hands. "What do you know of what the young men are doing, up there, as they work extra shifts?"

"Do you see that light bulb over there?" the old man asked.

Leo looked up. "Yes."

"The men from up on the mesa put the wires in last year. How did white men make electricity?"

Leo thought of all that he could say: of current, and charge, and electrons, and energy. He smiled. "It took a lot of doing," he said finally.

"That light bulb is the art of somebody who went out and observed his world," the old man said. "That world is what he captured."

Leo nodded and smiled.

They sat in silence.

The old man said, "You work up there."

Leo looked up, startled. "How did you know?"

"By observation," the old man said. "My granddaughter is invisible to her employers: to Miss Eleanor Garrigue, to the witch at La Posada, to the man who may have been watching you. And, I might add, to you."

Leo winced.

"But she is observant. She watches. She hears. You speak with an accent. You lie badly. And, of course, you walked around here, last year, with the other man, the one with the wire glasses. You looked, as I recall, as if you were visiting a zoo."

Leo, stunned, said nothing at first, then, "You know that no one can know this."

"Who would I tell?"

"I think there are a number of men, the man at the hotel, for one."

The old man said nothing. He stirred his coffee with a fork.

"Do you think I was followed here?" Leo asked.

"No," said the old man. "I don't think so. But I don't know. I am not a witch or a shaman. Or a Navajo—they always seem to know everything."

"What are you?"

"A man."

Griefa lifted the blanket at the door and looked in.

Leo, weary, waved to her.

She walked over to the stove and began slicing some kind of meat and putting it in a frying pan. A sticky-sweet smell rose to Leo's nose. She put the meat on a plate and served the two men. Leo looked at the pale pink meat with trepidation. The old man ate it with gusto. He looked up at Leo.

"White men captured electricity, and invented Spam," he said, with a little smile.

"What is Spam?" Leo asked.

"Bastard ham," the old man said solemnly, and returned to his plate.

Leo discovered he did not like Spam, but he ate it. Outside, he could still hear soft voices.

"What will you do about the dance?" he asked.

"Wait," the old man said, finishing his meal and wiping his hands on his jeans. Then, "Let's go outside."

Leo stepped under the blanket at the doorway and into the air outside. It was warmer, softer, more like summer suddenly. He and the old man were standing on the edge of the pueblo's plaza. Below

them were a few green fields with a ditch of brown water running
between them. Corn, the old man said. Leo let the sun warm his face.
He closed his eyes. When he opened them, the old man was studying him.

Leo turned away and watched a man crossing the ditch on a small
width of wood, his hair unbraided, the black wave swinging down his
back as he walked. Leo felt suddenly light-headed and turned, put
his hand against the wall behind him, and sat down.

"Are you getting ready to die?" asked the old man.

"No," Leo said, stubborn. "Not yet."

The old man nodded, looked down at the fields. Fat white clouds
moved across the deep blue sky.

"Do you pray?" asked the old man.

"No," said Leo.

"The woman Eleanor, she prays," the old man said.

"Yes," Leo said, curious.

"I have never fully understood the Christian religion," the old man
said.

"The only time I have liked that religion was when she talked
about it," said Leo.

"I like that," the old man said.

"Do you pray?" Leo asked.

"Yes."

"Who do you pray to?"

"To the wind. Sometimes the trees. Everything is made of everything else and can be changed into everything else. I pray to that.
And sometimes I pray not to die."

"If I prayed at all, I would pray for that."

"That, I think, is the origin of prayer."

Leo laughed. Then he grew serious. "The origin of prayer, also,
don't you think, is to break the silence. That someone will hear us."

The old man looked at him.

"That is your prayer," he said finally. And then, "I am going in to take a nap," and he turned and disappeared into the house. Leo sat against the wall with the sun on his face. The dirt wall behind his back was warm to the touch of his hand. It felt like a baked crust. He imagined the people living here for more than a thousand years, and their technologies: spears, hoes, knives, a rock on a sling. A knife-point of black chipped stone.

Cold air woke him up. The sun was going down and various people were standing on the edge of a round building in the center of the plaza to watch it. One was wrapped in a blanket. Others wore old hunting jackets, and one child was in a red knit sweater. Leo watched the setting sun light the bottoms of the clouds in pink. Slowly, feeling for the wall behind him, he stood up and walked back inside.

SIXTEEN

The pueblo in the morning was a tableau of mangy dogs, low fires, a boy carrying a lamb. Leo watched from the door of the old man's house. A group of women walked slowly toward the edge of the dirt plaza. Then an army bus pulled up and its doors folded open with a squeak. The half-days. Leo ducked back inside. The old man was sitting at the table drinking coffee into which he had poured a healthy dose of condensed milk.

"The women who work up there"—the old man gestured toward the door—"also say that everyone is working harder."

"That would be," Leo replied.

"The Germans are finished. So, why?"

"The Japanese."

"Ah," said the old man. He folded his hands. "Another kind of people." Then he said, "My granddaughter says you will not go back up there."

"No," Leo said. "That's no longer possible."

Griefa walked through the doorway and stood, hands behind her back, watching him.

"Can you get me to the train?" Leo asked.

"My brother's truck is broken," Griefa said. "He says he needs a battery."

"I've got to get to the train," Leo said.

"We can travel to Señora Eleanor's house in the cart, and I will ask to borrow the Ford automobile."

Leo frowned. "I don't think that's a good idea, Griefa," he said. Her face was impassive.

"It's the meal served to you," she said.

Leo shook his head. "I don't understand," he said. Then he turned to the old man. "Miss Garrigue is afraid of me. She may have told someone in Santa Fe about me. She certainly won't help me."

The two of them said nothing. Then the old man said, "My grand-daughter thinks Señora Eleanor regrets what she did."

Leo looked at Griefa. Griefa nodded, only slightly.

"What makes you think that?" Leo asked.

"After you left, the day after, she drove back into town," Griefa said, picking up a cup from the table. "In a hurry. I don't think she slept much."

"That is your evidence? On which I am supposed to base my future?" Leo said with scorn, suddenly weary of these queer, indirect people.

Griefa looked down at her shoes. She folded her arms across her chest. The old man looked away, trying to ignore his guest's rude behavior.

Leo threw up his hands and sighed. He wondered whether he could walk to Lamy, to the train station so far from anywhere.

"Well, I can hardly call a taxi," he said.

He followed Griefa outside, and she lifted up the tarp in the back of her cart and gestured to him. He climbed up and crawled under it. He smelled animals and hay, some kind of fuel. The tarp smelled of oil. She clucked to the horse.

He lay on his side and tried to let himself relax into the bumping roll, the motion of travel over dirt and rocks. He felt in danger once again, an extreme vulnerability. He rehearsed what to say to Eleanor

Garrigue. If he could find out who she had driven into town to see. Undoubtedly, the priest. Then he would beg her to take him to the train, no more questions asked. If he could keep her with him, she would not be able to warn anyone until he was on his way. If, if, if— and here the thought of seeing Eleanor Garrigue again intruded into his planning. He would see her face, and her clear, unyielding, very green eyes. He remembered standing over her, about to touch her shoulder.

The cart stopped and Leo smelled the damp scent of clay and willow. He heard the sound of the horse drinking, the whoosh of water blown through its huge soft nostrils. Griefa called his name, and he sat upright. She pulled the heavy tarp off him. They were parked beside the river, the pink plumes of tamarisk trees nearby. A cottonwood had sent its seeds floating like fluff in the wind; some of it caught in Leo's hair. The horse was standing with its front feet in the river, tossing its head back, forward, and back, like one of those toy drinking birds. He felt what the Germans called "nostalgia for a thing in the present that is passing," that this world was shortly to end, as all worlds end, as each of his worlds had ended, and so the present moment's sweetness was all the more acute.

"You can sit up front now," Griefa said stiffly.

"Thank you," Leo replied.

Griefa commanded the horse to move, and, with some balking, it turned away from the water. Leo looked across the river one last time and then turned his head away.

In the early evening light, Eleanor saw the cart coming up the driveway. She saw patches of sweaty fur on the horse under the harness. Griefa was wearing her hat with the plastic roses and a pair of gray leather and cloth gloves with wide cuffs, making her look vaguely like a musketeer. A figure sat beside Griefa.

Eleanor shaded her eyes. The hope in her that had faded and become parched now rose again. In the years to come, she would remember this particular moment in images of things: the heat of her *portal*, the wet patches of fur on the brown and black horse, the gloves that Griefa wore, bought by Eleanor from the Montgomery Ward catalog and given to Griefa at Christmas—icons of that moment, that day. Desire came back to her, as a new being, as a thing she could have. Desire as a bittersweet thirst.

Leo climbed down off the wagon, and it creaked as he moved. His left hand held the seat for balance. As he reached the ground, a puff of dust. Rita bounded over to him, barking, and he stopped. She ambled over and smelled his hand, then nudged him on the knee, and he reached down to pat her speckled head before he looked up at Eleanor.

There were sounds, coming from a few directions. Griefa clicked at the horse and it snorted in irritated reply. The harness clacked against itself; the horse swished its tail at flies. Eleanor did not move.

Griefa must have climbed down herself at some point, because when Eleanor looked over at the cart again, Griefa was holding the horse's head and leading him toward the *acequia* to drink. Leo walked toward Eleanor. He walked solemnly, one foot in front of the other on the graveled ground. She simply watched him. His shirt was pressed against his body, and his hair was dark and had something in it, some white halo of fluff.

She moved her hands to her thighs. She stayed as still as she could.

Leo saw her standing there from a way off, lit by the light of the house behind her. All of what he had planned to do and say floated out of his mind. He let himself move toward her.

She backed away as he came up the walk. Neither of them saw Griefa climb back onto the cart's seat and turn the horse away from the gate. Eleanor backed into the house, as if seeking some kind of privacy, as Leo walked toward her, and she backed away. She was wearing a pale blue shirt and a skirt, a silver bracelet on her narrow wrist. He tried to find just the right words.

"I have things to tell you," he said. "I am sorry I didn't tell you earlier."

She said something, whispered something.

He reached toward her, but she backed away. She said, "Who are you?" This asked with real fear in it, with urgency.

"My name is Leo Kavan," he said. "I am a physicist," he said, and laughed, too tensely, he noted, and added, "hot, dirty, and world renowned."

She moved backward and he moved forward, as if they were one of those crazy pairs of dolls on a wood slider.

"A physicist," she said. "I only know of Einstein."

"My professor," Leo replied. "Please, tell me. Have you told anyone of my presence here?"

"Yes," she said sadly, and his heart dropped. "I told my minister, Father Bill Taylor. But the next morning, after you left, I told him not to tell anyone. To keep you a secret."

"Is he good at keeping secrets?"

"He is a priest," she said, affronted.

That will have to do, Leo thought.

"What are you doing here?" She felt itchy, odd, inexpert.

"Oh my dear," he replied. "That is a long story."

"Isn't it time you began?"

He saw the whole house this time, as if from the other end of a kaleidoscope. He passed through the door into the kitchen. He took in the table by the window, the geraniums on the windowsill above the sink, the wooden bowl with its hasp. And something that wasn't there before: a photo of a young man in a uniform on the bureau, and a tall candle in a glass in front of it. He stopped. Eleanor turned. Leo looked over at her, to see her eyes.

They were now in the living room, out of the kitchen. He could see behind her shoulder the wide bedlike couch. It had a lovely proximity. It looked more or less like an island, he thought. Like one of those islands he had read about in books as a child. White sand, turquoise waters, palm trees. Nothing he had actually seen in his life.

"Are you a spy?" she asked softly, and he realized that was what she had made of the letter to Felix.

"No," he replied almost impatiently. "Not a spy. You must believe me. I really am a physicist, born in Czechoslovakia. You placed the accent." He reached for her hand, suddenly, without knowing he was going to, but she retreated.

"I found something, on my desk . . ."

"Yes, very stupid," he said. "But needed, necessary." He paused, letting space come between them, knowing that something must be said to let her into his world, and thus to implicate her. He was on the verge of a great precipice, looking down into a gulf he couldn't measure. He must let this woman into his life, and therefore put her in jeopardy.

"It was a letter," he said stupidly. Then, "Someone has to do something." She heard the urgency and the gravity in his voice, and some terrible thing pressed against her, as if a blot of darkness had entered the room behind him.

"You are hot," she said. She felt so awkward, not knowing how to make the next step. Now they were both in front of the fireplace.

"I can't," she said. And he felt completely bereft.

"I can't know everything," she said. "But I have to know something. You have to give me something. It's too hard, otherwise." She shook her head as if shaking away a fly.

"Everything I tell you," he said, "might put you in the place where I am, where I have been living. It is not only the"—he stopped for a second—"the others. It's the place where I am." He thought of getting up in the morning, placing the slide rule in his pocket like an automaton, and the sleepless nights.

Then he said, simply, "I want to tell you what I know." Then he started again, and finally said, "I want—" He could feel the warmth of her body within inches of his. She whispered something.

"What is that?" he asked.

"It was here, all the time," she said. "Or was it here? Did you know?"

She reached up and tried to flick the cottonwood fluff out of his hair. As her hands touched his head, her body touched his shirt. He shivered and his arms went around her. He placed his hands on her back and pulled her toward him with all he had in him. They stopped for a second like that, a measure of time, as if each movement had to have its repose.

He folded her against him, hooked one leg around hers so that he could feel her hips and the long length of her leg. He moved his mouth along her jaw, and then moved her head so that he could find her lips, and kissed her for the first time.

She kissed him, and she felt a tension finally assuaged. At last this thing her mouth had wanted, this completed act. His mouth was strong and she felt that she could follow its lead; she could let herself flow into him through her mouth. His tongue touched hers, gently, awkwardly, and then again, this time with greater ease and authority. She moved her hands down his back, followed his spine, the knobs of bone and then flesh.

She began to soften against him, to feel herself opening. Part of her wanted to call herself back, away from the edge, but her body had found itself, leaning against him. He moved her gently toward the couch until they were beside it.

"How did you get here, to New Mexico?" she asked.

"By train," he replied, and laughed.

It was so slow, as if she were swimming in a large lake. He did nothing quickly. She felt a sense of slow relaxing into him, against him, of knowing him. Her body relaxed before her mind knew what had happened. They were traveling. She moved her hands under his shirt, and she felt his warm skin. She was moving into water, swimming through a lake's clear, heavy atmosphere, her arms weightless, only the deep pull of moving toward him as an orientation. She swam, and he swam with her. He opened her shirt one button at a time. Wait, wait, he told himself as she rose toward him. He folded his hand under her and pulled off her skirt until he had freed her of her clothes. Slowly, he said to himself, somewhere in the back of his mind, slowly. He thought of an old math equation, shoe polish, a crust of bread. Fragments of thoughts floated in her mind—her canoe in its slip at the dock, rocking in the water, a pink linen dress. It was like an ache now; she would not be able to stand it much longer, and she felt him move his hands under her, gripping her. One hand parted her legs. It was not possible, she thought, to hold this pleasure as he rose over her. He found her, her hips lifted off the bed, her voice unknown to her, whispered, called, began to sound.

SEVENTEEN

A dry, warm wind blew out of the canyons onto Los Alamos, withering the new irises and crocus. After the April snows, the usual spring afternoon rains had not arrived. The hillsides already had a faded, desperate look. As David walked past Kistiakowsky's stone house toward S-site, dust rose from his feet. The mood on the Hill was all work. There were no parties anymore. The men often stayed all night in the labs, and everyone was secretive and silent. The secrets before this had leaked like water through a sieve, and he had had no trouble passing on to Naomi and she to her brother all of what needed to be shared. But not now. Just last night, he witnessed how much worry there was over spies when half the town was out with binoculars watching a bright object in the sky. It took the head of Personnel, an amateur astronomer, to calm their nerves by explaining to everyone that it would not be wise to try to shoot down the planet Venus.

As he walked past the east mess hall, he heard someone say a forest fire had broken out in the night. The water situation was so tight that one of the WACS said she was brushing her teeth with Coca-Cola.

David knew why the tension was high, and why the scientists were suddenly buttoned down. The gadget itself was moving from theory to reality, taking those final steps from men's minds through their hands, to be birthed into the world of real things. David imagined this process as he walked along the rutted road, how Einstein saw the atom, and Leo Kavan the energy released from a nucleus, and so on and so on, and how once something was imagined, men desired to make it. This is our gift, our desire, to see a thing in the world that was once only in our minds. We cannot stop ourselves.

But the plutonium bomb had to be tested before it was dropped on a city: implosion was theoretical. They had to scrape together enough plutonium for two implosion bombs: one to test in the desert, where if things went wrong nothing would be missed, and one to fall from an airplane. Not on a German city. Not anymore. David wondered if they were choosing that place. Who would choose?

David's frustration at being unable to crack the secret of the location and date of the test of the gadget ate at him. Naomi said her brother had said he would come out from Brooklyn "if that's what it takes," as if David weren't capable of solving this particular problem on his own. As if Peter would be of any use sitting in an apartment in Albuquerque. David shook his head. Nevertheless, the truth was, he had gotten nowhere, and time was running out. Frank Oppenheimer had disappeared from the Hill.

The riddle of Dr. Kavan was like static in the back of his mind. Slotin had committed suicide, someone said. Someone else said no, that wasn't possible. He was in the army hospital in Bethesda, being treated for nervous shock. But nothing about Dr. Kavan. Nothing at all.

Other rumors had sifted down to David's level. Ever since Hitler's suicide on the last day of April, scientists in the Tech Area, those with white badges, had been meeting privately. As David walked past them on his way to the dining hall, Emilio Segre said to Robert Wilson, chief of the experimental physics division, "Now that the bomb cannot be used against the Nazis, I have my doubts."

Wilson nodded. "I thought we were fighting the Nazis," he said, "not the Japanese particularly."

A few days later, Wilson plastered the lab halls with notices for a meeting on "The Impact of the Gadget on Civilization" to be held in the cyclotron building. David heard that twenty men had turned up to talk that night about why they were continuing to make the bomb after the war against the Germans had been virtually won. No one, someone had pointed out, thought the Japanese had a bomb program.

David's friend told him that Oppenheimer had arrived late at the meeting and the men had turned toward him, hoping for an answer. It was not up to scientists to make political decisions, he had said. "If you are a scientist, you cannot stop such a thing." Besides, they needed to keep working so that the bomb could be tested. The world needed to know about the new weapon; it would change the world, and end war as they knew it. That seemed to end the discussion, and the men had gone home to sleep and work another day.

David walked inside and began melting down the high explosive. He liked the early morning, when he was alone and the air was still free of fumes. He was careful. He paid attention. The point was to be so particular that you didn't make any mistakes. Generally, David had noticed, people were not as vigilant as he was. Their minds wandered. They stayed up too late and took too many breaks. It was like chess: know the pieces, watch your opponent for the moment when his attention wanders, and then you win.

Kistiakowsky marched in. Under his eyes were great dark shadows. David wondered how long he had been there or if he had gone back to his bed at all last night. "These things are giving me the greatest agony," he said to David as he passed him. David nodded and continued to work, hoping to present a casual nonchalance. In a little while, he looked up to see Kistiakowsky outside pacing, as usual. When Kistiakowsky walked back inside, David turned and, to his own dismay, blurted out, "What is the hurry? Are we nearing the test?"

Kistiakowsky smiled at him. "You work so hard, David. You are so good at what you do. You know we are getting near, and these molds still crack."

David tried to smile back, but tension forced his mouth into a grimace. "I am . . . out of touch with the conclusion of my work."

"Yes," Kistiakowsky said quietly. "I don't like it any more than you do." He added, with a smirk, "But we're in the army now!"

David frowned, turning back to the kettle in front of him. Then he put down his tools and decided. It was simple, really. It had an elegance to it. He walked over to Kistiakowsky and asked him for a day off. To see Naomi. Kistiakowsky frowned.

"It's not a good time, David."

"I have been working for many weekends," David said. "More than the rest."

"That's true," Kistiakowsky said. "You have worked hard. But can't it wait?"

David slumped his shoulders and sulked. He knew that Kistiakowsky liked to keep everyone happy. He was about to turn back to his work, in silence, when Kistiakowsky said, "Okay. Just a day."

When they were alone that night, Kistiakowsky pushed into the room a machine with pulleys and arms that David finally recognized as a dentist's drill.

"Go home, Davey," Kistiakowsky said. "Get some sleep."

"What are you going to do?"

Kistiakowsky smiled. "Dental work," he said. "We have to fill some cavities."

He placed a mold in his lap and maneuvered the drill into position.

David backed away.

"Good night, Davey," Kistiakowsky said.

"Aren't you afraid?"

"No," Kistiakowsky said. "If it blows in my lap, I'll never know it."

EIGHTEEN

Eleanor woke in the dark, hungry and thirsty, and slid off the couch. She slipped a glass under the faucet and ran water into it. She drank, standing barefoot on the floor, and opened a window to breathe in the smell of the night. Every part of her body felt alive. *"I get no kick from champagne,"* she sang softly to herself. *"Mere alcohol doesn't thrill me at all. But I . . ."* Rita pushed her nose into Eleanor's palm.

When Leo opened his eyes in the morning, he couldn't place for a second where he was. He rolled over and looked out into the room. His pants were on the floor, and he felt what must be her shirt somewhere near his feet. Sometime in the night, she must have placed a blanket over them. After making love, he thought, there is always this embarrassing disarray. He heard her at the sink, and then she moved into his view, wrapped in flannel, and he felt a flood of tenderness and desire for her, and a bolt of fear because of the peril he had placed her in.

Eleanor made eggs and Leo sat at the window. He watched as she knocked each egg against the side of the bowl with one hand and allowed the eggs to drop into a glass bowl while holding the crumpled shell.

"How do you do that?" he asked.

"It's all in the wrist," she replied.

She looked over at him. He was gazing out the window. His shirt was open at the throat. He ran his hand over his chin. She wondered what he was thinking about.

She had overcooked the eggs. Quickly she scraped them out of the pan, considered making them all over again, and judged against it. She put them on two china plates, her grandmother's Spode with pale green birds flitting in and out of flowering trees, opened the oven door, and pulled out the cooked bacon on its bed of paper. She removed the flour tortillas from the oven as well, the ones Griefa had made for her, and wrapped them in a clean white dishtowel. She took the silver from a drawer, her mother's Gorham, and two placemats and brought them over to him. She placed them on the table and said, "Will you set the table?"

"What are these called again?" he asked, holding up the placemat. She told him.

"Place Mat," he said, putting it down on the table and arranging the silver on the top. "Place Mat."

She set the plates down; he thanked her. She sat down.

"What is *implosion*?" she asked.

Leo put down his fork. "Where did you hear that word?"

"You said it," she said, put off by his tone. "You said it the night I brought you here from the river."

"In my sleep?"

"In your delirium," she said.

"What do you think it means?" he asked, more gently.

"The opposite of *explosion*?"

"Right on the dime," he said.

"Right on the money," she said, and smiled.

"Right on the money," he repeated.

"But it's specific, isn't it?" She couldn't let it go. "I mean, it means something specific. You didn't simply use a word no one uses that is the opposite of *explosion* in your sleep."

"It's specific," he said, irritated.

She saw his irritation and grew irritated herself; she shoved herself back from the table.

"I'll wash the dishes," she said, getting up.

He watched her move across the kitchen floor, her back stiff with hurt and irritation. "*Implosion* is a specific way of describing an experimental situation in which a . . . a gadget releases energy inward rather than outward, causing a reaction in which a greater release of energy than the constituted parts would normally . . ." Leo stopped.

Eleanor turned. She walked back over to the table and said, "Say that again."

"*Implosion* describes a theoretical situation in which shock waves travel inward, causing a . . ." Leo stopped, then added, "Causing another event to take place."

"Does this have anything to do with rockets?"

Leo laughed. "I believe Dr. Service, Mr. Service, went to the La Fonda bar one night to spread a rumor around about electric rockets. He found only a drunk carpenter who wanted to dance with him and talk about sheep. He didn't think he was successful."

"So, it's not rockets."

"No," Leo said sadly. "Not of any sort."

A silence. She waited. "Or submarines? I have also heard submarines."

"I went to work on this project to stop the Germans," Leo said, ducking the question she had implied. "That's what I told myself, at least."

"They seem to be stopped," she said quietly.

"They are stopped," he replied.

"What about the Japanese?" Her voice rose.

"They are not, yet," he said. He searched her face.

"My brother is in the Pacific," she said.

"I remember."

"Is what you are"—she stopped to correct herself—"were working on to defeat the Nazis—could it stop the Japs?"

Leo was silent. He thought of the words he had written in his letter to Roosevelt: "Please exercise your power as commander in chief . . ."

"Yes," he replied.

"Good," she replied. "The sooner the better. My brother is starving."

Leo pushed back his chair. Where was her brother? He worried, once again, whether they would take the proximity of a prison camp into consideration if and when they chose a target.

"Do you know where your brother is, I mean exactly?"

"No," she said. "Why?"

"Oh, nothing, really," Leo lied. "I simply wondered."

"You might be a madman," she said, "with grandiose ideas."

"I am both," Leo replied. He remembered Frisch turning to him at dinner when he had thought about dropping the slug through the center of the mass. "Is it really crazy enough?"

"Is someone looking for you?" she asked.

"I don't know," he replied. "But, yes, probably, by now."

In the bright morning, Leo and Eleanor walked out into the sun and down toward the arroyo, Rita trotting ahead, her ears turning back when they spoke. Leo drew fresh air into his lungs. Layers of pine needles lined the driveway as if a basket were woven along its length. He thought about how last night he had been carried down this road in a battered wagon and now it was as if the world had been remade overnight.

He followed her onto the arroyo's floor. He noticed that she had a long, uneven stride, that she swung her arms as she walked. Reddish clay was exposed on a bank. He saw that Eleanor had entered into this world completely, that she was no longer pitched to him. The dog had a wet black nose. He felt a distant relation to his life of the last two years and happily pondered whether he, alone among men, had survived Einstein's bridge to another universe: Here, a dry creek bed beloved to a woman, a dog, a bowl with a copper hasp, laundry, a bed. Up there, U-235, a detonation wave, a developing implosion, the most expensive scientific project in the world.

He slipped on a rock and caught himself on a branch just before falling on top of her.

"I am dangerous." He laughed as he righted himself.

She turned.

"Leo," she said, "why did you leave your work?"

"There was an accident." He stopped. He heard in his mind the sound of Slotin's screams.

"Yes?" she asked.

"My best friend was killed."

"Oh," she said. "Leo, I am sorry."

"Yes, thank you. We were working together. Dangerous work. There was an accident. And he saved my life by losing his."

She was standing with her arms folded, her eyes on his face.

He looked down at her. "I was ill, when you found me, from this accident. Do you remember when you asked me about a doctor?"

Eleanor nodded.

"I told you it was a new ailment."

"As new as its cause."

"Right on the money." He could see she was waiting.

"It was an exposure. Too much of a thing, a kind of poison. But I may be all right, after all. It's not easy to know."

"Because it is new."

"Yes."

She was looking up at him. He studied her face.

"Isn't there a way to know? If you found the right doctor?"

"No, Eleanor," Leo said softly.

"Okay," she replied, solemn. "And after the accident? You left?"

"I left, yes, after the accident. I was ill, but I got stronger. Not strong enough, as it happened. I thought I would drown, swimming across that river. I left because . . . because I had a . . . What is the expression? A change of blood?"

"A change of heart."

"Exactly. That's what I had. My heart changed. And so I left, without formal permission. I am a stubborn man. I did not want to ask."

"And now?"

"And now, Eleanor," he said, "we have today."

Rita barked, and they turned away from each other.

"I have told you a small portion of my life," Leo said. "Tell me something of yours."

"I was born in Chicago."

"A good city."

"You know it?"

"I worked there."

"Where?" she asked.

"Under the football field at the university. I am interrupting you."

"My father was an architect. He designed many of the buildings in the city. The Zoological Gardens. St. Chrysostom's Church. He used to take me on little tours, showing me buildings. We lived in the suburbs, and we traveled. We traveled often to Prague." She stopped. She had not told her story to anyone for a long time. "That is why I thought I heard Czech in your accent."

"Prague," he said, and remembered the newspaper clipping in her desk. "You are related to Charlotte Garrigue Masaryk."

"Yes," she said. "My father's aunt."

"My God," he replied. "How amazing that I would have found you, of all people, here."

"I, actually, was the one who found you."

"Czech, mate," Leo said, grinning.

"Oh, God," Eleanor said, and hit him on the arm.

"Did you learn to paint in Chicago?"

"Yes, there and in New York."

"I don't think I have ever known a woman painter."

Eleanor sighed. "I wish it were just 'painter' without the 'woman' attached."

"When there are more of you, then that will be the case," Leo said calmly. "I studied with a 'woman' physicist, Dr. Meitner, Lise, in Berlin. I also worked with her nephew, Dr. Frisch . . ." He paused. He had been about to say "here." He found himself on the verge of chatter, having had no one outside the Project to talk to.

Eleanor wanted to ask him, What was the work? Where did you study? But she had seen what it did to him to refuse her. Instead she said, "Was it easy for her? To be a woman and a scientist?"

"I don't know. It didn't occur to me."

"What is physics, anyway? I have never understood. "

"You could think of it as the study of matter and energy. Or, as Griefa's grandfather would say, the science of those who observe the world, and what they capture. But my favorite is the one my teacher Dr. Meitner used. It was this: 'Physics is a battle for final truth.' "

"The battle is to find the truth?"

"A truth. Even a *final* truth, but not *the* truth. Because once you found what you thought was the truth, another, more 'final' truth will come along, sooner or later."

"To distinguish physics from religion."

"Yes, perfectly, right on the money."

Leo brushed away a branch.

"How do you think about painting?" he asked. "I mean, how did you manage to make that painting in the bedroom?"

"Oh, that's a very hard question. Sometimes I think of it as break-ing things up into their parts or their shapes, or their essences, as

Kandinsky would say. Getting down to the shapes of things, and a kind of odd dynamic or interaction among shapes. You know, I anchor a scene in reality, so to speak, as I did with the figure, but then as I paint, the shapes themselves start to speak. It's funny, it's as if things had their own energy below what we see normally and I'm trying to grasp it, see it, and paint it."

Leo looked at her. "That's astonishing. Because . . ." He paused. "Well, things *do* have what you call energy, at another level. Things are all moving at a subatomic level, constantly."

"Do they interact?"

"Yes," he said sadly. "Yes, they do. Especially if we help them along."

Eleanor saw his mood darken, and she was silent. She walked on the snowy ground, relishing the air on her face. Then she turned to him.

"Leo, besides your sister, is the rest of your family still in Prague?"

Leo looked at her and tried to soften his tone. "We are Jewish, Eleanor. None of us are left there."

"Do you know where they are?" she asked.

"In the wind," Leo said. Then he stopped. He had to stop.

In the cool evening, Eleanor made a fire in the bedroom. Taking kindling from the basket near the hearth, she made a small teepee with three sticks the way her father taught her. She was aware of his presence behind her. She turned, stood up, and lifted her eyes. He was standing near the door, watching her.

"What are you going to do?"

"I am going to watch you make a fire."

"I mean in the long run."

"I know what you mean."

She felt the thickness of desire in her throat.

. . .

As she came back into the room, she saw him smoking in the dark.

"Are Czechs famous for their prowess in bed?"

"For generations," he replied.

He leaned his back against the wall. "In England where I worked, there was a man Guy, the son of a gun merchant and a lady-in-waiting to the English queen."

Eleanor climbed back into the bed, and Rita hopped up and settled herself against Leo's hip. "He told me one night," Leo said as he fitted Eleanor's head against his shoulder, " 'You Czechs are like visitors from Mars. Everyone knows that Martians have difficulty speaking without an accent that would give them away. So they pretend to be Czech, whose inability to speak any language except Czech without an accent is legendary.' "

Leo laughed into the dark. "There were eight of us Martians. We were known for our prowess in bed and our ability to do math."

He looked down at her, and then he remembered what he had found beside the newspaper clipping in the desk drawer. The photograph of the man, and Eleanor in white.

"One more thing," Leo said.

"Yep," Eleanor replied.

"I saw a photo of you in your desk. You were carrying flowers. Next to a man, a striking sort of man, with a brush mustache."

Eleanor left his arms so quickly, he almost lunged for her.

"My husband," she said.

NINETEEN

In La Fonda's courtyard, Bill stirred his coffee with the hotel's silver-plated spoon. Lydia had offered him eggs and bacon, but he had turned her down. A nostalgia for the East swept through him, how he used to leave the seminary close and be carried into the wave of life on the streets of New York in minutes. He once heard a sewer man, his hand held high as if wielding a sword, yell out before disappearing into the bowels of the street, "Once more into the breach, dear friends!" But he had grown fond of this place, fond of La Fonda.

When he had collected his mail earlier that week, he had found among the letters an envelope marked with David's now familiar scrawl. David wanted to have a game earlier than usual. On the weekend.

Why not, Bill had thought, and he had written a quick reply. Now he turned to see David hunch his way across the lobby, his small eyes squinting as he crossed the expanse of tiled floor, a thing to be conquered. "Once more into the breach, dear friends," Bill said, chuckling, and then wondered, suddenly, if David was what Bill had always taken him for, a precise technician of some kind.

David arrived at the table, pulled out a chair, grunted at Bill, nodded to Lydia, and sat down.

"It's important," David said without preliminaries. "I want to talk to him."

"To whom?" Bill said.

"To the man your parishioner found by the river," David snorted. "Your"—he paused, and then enunciated syllable by syllable—"your pa-ri-shion-er's friend."

Lydia arrived with a coffeepot. Her scar looked more visible, Bill thought.

She poured into David's cup, and he took it up in his paws and drank.

"I don't understand," Bill said. "I don't know even where he is. And you were not interested in him. You did not even think you knew him, before."

"I would like to talk to him," David said. "About our business, his and mine."

"What is your business, David?"

"It's war-related, as I have told you."

"So you, and this man, both of you are in the same work?"

"Possibly. In different areas of the same work."

Bill's hands were jumpy, so he folded them together. What harm in this? Get them together to do whatever they need to do, and get her out of it. Whatever it is.

"Look," Bill began. Then hesitated. "Look," he said. "I don't want to play games. Is she in any danger?"

"Not from him," David replied. "Not from him."

"Whatever do you mean?"

"I mean that his work is so secret that if she is found to be with him, if he is found to be, well, AWOL . . ." David floated his hand in the air beside the table. "CCI," he said. "FBI."

Bill stared at David's hand. He felt slow to understand, as if David had switched to another language, German, perhaps, or French.

"I can't find my way through this, David," he said. "You'll have to tell me more."

"I would like to talk to him," David repeated, rubbing his hand along his thigh. He is shining, Bill thought. He is shining with a thought, with a scheme, with a plan. For the first time, Bill was afraid of him.

"Do you think you could tell him, if you happened to see him, that David Stein wants to talk to him?"

"I don't like this," Bill replied.

"And, meanwhile," David said, "I won't tell anyone you know something. Meanwhile." And he rose from the table, threw a few coins down, and began to walk away.

Bill stood up. "I'll call you later and let you know."

"That's impossible," David said, returning to the table. Lowering his voice to a harsh whisper, he said, "You cannot call me. Contact her, and then let me know by mail. Then we will all know together, the same thing."

"It could take a while," Bill said.

David looked at him, measuring him.

"I'll meet you at your office in six days," he said, and walked away.

Bill walked out of the lobby, turned right, and walked up the street, past the statue of Archbishop Lamy and then up East Palace toward the church offices, past La Posada's *portal* and the small man who sat outside selling newspapers and gum. Bill went into the office, smiled at Lou, the office volunteer that day, a portly woman with an intelligent face who wrote poetry, sent it to East Coast journals, and received short handwritten rejections in return. He marched into the sacristy, where he pulled a flask from under the Easter linen, took a pull, and replaced it. He took a stole from the collection hanging over a pole in the closet. As he kissed the cross in the center, he wondered how many times he had kissed this spot, more often than a woman's lips, and placed it over his head, adjusting it with both hands. He grasped each side of the fabric as he walked into the church, then selected a pew and pulled the kneeler down.

TWENTY

When news of the German surrender reached Santa Fe, Eleanor was stretching a canvas in the living room. She had cleared her father's desk of the crystal paperweight and ink well, blotter and pen stand, and covered the surface with a clean white cloth. Then she laid the heavy linen on top of it, and the frame over that. She placed her mallet and a set of copper tacks on the desk. She stood over them, hands on her hips. Behind her, the radio was playing Gershwin. She put a tack between her teeth and pulled the linen taut in the middle of one side. Once it was tight, she took the tack out of her mouth, placed its sharp end against the linen-swathed wood, and tapped at it with her mallet. She sighed. Even if the painting went badly, the pure mechanics of preparation pleased her. She walked around the desk, pulled the linen from the opposite side, placed the tack, tapped it, and the tack went in.

Leo was outside the house, sitting on the *portal* in the sun, reading. When she got the four sides of the canvas fixed, she walked over to the kitchen's open door to take a look at him. He held the book—Whitman's *Leaves of Grass*—in his left hand; his mouth was relaxed. She loved to look at him like this, without his knowing. In these few days they had had together, they had settled into a domestic rhythm; it filled her with pleasure to pretend to take him for granted. She brushed her mouth with the back of her hand and felt his lips. They had not talked about her marriage for very long. He had said, "Ah," when she had said, "My husband." Then he had said, "I thought so." And she had said, "Yes." Then he had said, "Where is he?" And she had said, "I don't know." After a brief silence, he had said, rueful, "So you had a secret, too."

An announcer broke into the music. He had a grating, high-pitched voice, and she turned from her work. "Germany gives up!" he cried. "The Nazi banner is now struck to earth, nevermore to fly again in a world of peace-loving nations."

Eleanor rushed to the door and called to Leo, who stood up with the book in his hand and walked quickly inside. They stood together, their heads bowed to the radio. She still held the hammer in one hand. General Eisenhower had accepted the Germans' unconditional surrender in Reims. The Germans were to surrender their arms, their ships were to return to port, there was to be no scuttling of a vessel, no harm done to a hull, no destruction of a warehouse or weapon. The surrender was written in German and in English; the English version would be the "authentic" text.

"Every *t* crossed," Eleanor said.

"What?"

"Too hard to explain," she said, and laughed.

He held out his arms to her. She put down the hammer and climbed into them, and they began to dance, as the radio played Glenn Miller's band, an ode to the musician who had lost his life over the English Channel. Leo spun her around the room, his feet moving in circles and hers flying after him. Rita, barking, pounced at their feet and knocked over a chair. Eleanor drew back her head.

"What are we dancing?"

"A polka. My grandmother's favorite gentile invention."

They flung themselves on the couch and Leo wiped his forehead with the tail of his shirt. Eleanor leaned against him, hip to hip.

She turned toward him and looked into his face.

"Will they be able to find your sister now?"

He frowned and smoothed her hair.

"I hope so."

Eleanor's thoughts were of Teddy, and the lack of letters, the nearness of her hope and its extinction.

"Leo," she said, "what of Japan?"

He looked into the space in the middle of the room. "If the project I was working on succeeds, Japan will be destroyed," he said finally. "In its entirety."

"That will end that war, too," she said. "I want an end to that war. I want my brother to come home."

Leo thought about Lotte and his desire to keep her safe at every cost. How he had worked on the Project to save her life. Where she might be in the ruins of Europe.

"I know how much you want him home," he said. "But the Japanese are not the German army. They are close to finality. And they have never been working on a . . ." He had very nearly said it.

She glanced at him.

"They say the war could go on with them for months. He may not have months. If your project could end it sooner, then I don't understand why." She sat up.

He put a hand on her back. "I don't tell you not out of stubbornness but because of the danger it would put you in to know. I am one of those responsible for its creation, and I have turned against it: my own Frankenstein monster. It will consume everything in its path."

She heard his tone. She turned to look at his face.

She put her hand on his hand and held her hand flat on top of his, matching her fingers to his.

"Eleanor, believe me," he said.

"I believe you. I don't understand. I can't, really. But I believe you."

Leo sighed. "I had not realized how much that would matter to me."

Eleanor smiled. "I'm glad it matters to you."

It was like walking on a tightrope toward each other.

"We each have secrets," Eleanor said. "I suppose we will have to forgive each other for our secret lives. It seems to me it is required."

He took her in his arms and kissed her. "Thank you," he said. Then, "I know how much you love your brother. I will do everything I can."

Then, almost at the same time, they heard someone walk up the steps and across the *portal*, a tap on the door. Edgar flashed through Eleanor's mind, and Leo looked over at her, a question in his eyes. Then they both stood up and straightened their shoulders, as if coming through a membrane, as if they had to put on skin. Leo moved in front of Eleanor.

Griefa called from the door, "Señora Garrigue?"

"Good morning, Griefa," Eleanor said, wondering what brought her here.

"*Bueno,*" Griefa said. "May I come in?"

Eleanor took Leo's hand. He nodded and shrugged.

"Yes, please. Come in," Eleanor said. She released Leo's hand and moved toward the door. Griefa was crossing the threshold.

"Coffee?"

"No, *gracias.*"

Griefa stepped into the kitchen. "The man, this Leo," she said quickly.

"Yes?" Eleanor said.

"Hello, Griefa," he said.

"*Bueno,*" she replied.

"My friend Lydia, who works at La Fonda," Griefa said.

"Yes," Eleanor replied.

"There is a man, David, who works . . ." Griefa gestured toward the mesa that rose up in the distance.

"Where I work?" Leo said.

"Yes," Griefa said. "Where you work."

"David who?" Leo said.

"Stein," Griefa said.

The machinist, Leo thought. Penny-in-the-Slot Stein. And he remembered the night they'd played murder at Laura Fermi's house.

"How do you know that?" Leo asked.

"Lydia watches him," she replied.

Leo winced. "How many people does Lydia watch?"

"Only him," Griefa said.

"For how much?"

Griefa snorted. "That is not your question to ask. Do you wish to buy food for her children?"

Leo looked at his hands.

Eleanor was silent, her throat tightening.

"Lydia has seen David talking to the Episcopal father."

"To Father Bill?" Eleanor asked.

"To Padre Bill."

"Why Bill?"

"They play chess, on Saturdays."

"Oh," Eleanor said.

Leo leaned forward.

"And?"

"And they have been talking about you," Griefa said, looking at Leo.

Leo looked away.

Miserably, Eleanor said, "But I told him to keep you a secret! I told him not to speak of you!"

Leo nodded, his heart faint in his chest.

Griefa looked from one to the other, then her eyes rested on Leo. "David is asking where you are, to talk to you."

He rubbed his jaw with his hand. Eleanor stood up. "Griefa," she said, "please leave us alone, for now."

Leo turned around. He was standing in the living room near the couch when she came in.

"Leo," she said. He turned, his face a half-moon. "It isn't enough to say I am sorry."

"You had no idea," he said. "I didn't tell you enough. Or anything, for that matter. But who is this priest? Why is he speaking of things you asked him not to speak of?" Leo scowled. "Doesn't anyone in this country understand consequences?"

He turned, finally, all the way toward her. "It's happening as we stand here. They are moving forward. If I am arrested or detained . . . I am one of the very few who might stop it."

She stood very still.

"What will you do?" she said quickly, as if diving into cold water, all at once, so as not to have to feel it slowly.

Leo ran his hand through his hair. "I fear my timing is off."

He thought, but did not say, And the problem now is what might happen to you. And the complication, so to speak, of you and me.

Eleanor was quiet. She felt in herself the long distances they had traveled to find each other and the histories that could not be erased.

"I drove into town that day because I was suddenly afraid," she said. "I thought I was afraid you were a spy; that's what I told myself. But later, in the night, I realized it was me I was afraid of. I was afraid of what I felt. But I am not afraid of that anymore."

"Neither am I."

"Leo," she said firmly. "I will go into town and try to talk to Bill. He's a friend. I will tell him he must be silent."

She turned away to pick up her things, then turned back.

"And you?"

"I must get to the train."

"I know. Griefa can take you."

"In a cart?"

"It's the meal given you. That's what we have."

She put her hands on his chest and gathered his shirt into her hands.

TWENTY-ONE

Bill thanked God for the morning, a soft late spring day. A day on which he had had breakfast in the kitchen, a perfect breakfast of scrambled eggs and green chile, chiles he had grown himself last year, harvested, and frozen after roasting in the oven and peeling. Chile verde, the brilliant green kind, in thin skinless strips, and the eggs cooked in a little butter and oil the way his mother's cook made them, having studied under a chef from Italy. Toast, Dundee's marmalade, his father's favorite. Ever since Mrs. Stanley's confession, he had been thinking.

Mrs. Stanley had said she had lust.

Bill couldn't stop himself. "Lust for whom?" he had asked. He remembered the first confession he had heard, from a twelve-year-old who took him aside and whispered that she wanted to confess to adultery.

"Adultery!" Bill had blurted out.

"Yes," she'd said calmly. "Adultery. Disobeying an adult."

Lust, Mrs. Stanley had said, for the postman. She waited for him to come up the walk. His arms were muscular under his postman shirt. Oh, Lord, Bill thought, spare us the details. And lust for someone else, she said, unnamed. She was sitting behind Bill in the pew with the lily of the valley kneeler. He, in the pew in front of her, stared at the cross and thought about whether Jesus had had to do this kind of thing, between miracles. And I have been jealous, she said. Of certain unnamed persons in the congregation. "Ah," he said, wishing he could dispense a few Hail Marys and be done with it.

"Shall I say of whom I am jealous?" she asked.

"No," Bill replied, quickly. "It's all right. The jealousy itself is what matters. The jealousy," he heard himself say, "is the demon that binds you."

He heard Mrs. Stanley suck in her breath.

"Perhaps *demon* is too strong a word," he said. "Let us just say it is the thing that comes between you and God, which is the definition of sin."

Mrs. Stanley shifted her weight.

"Yes," she said, "the demon between me and God," warming to the idea. "Do you think it's possible?" She breathed heavily—Mrs. Stanley suffered from asthma. "For me to overcome this demon? Our Lord says that sins are to be forgiven, if they are repented."

"Of course," Bill said sharply. Mrs. Stanley sat back; Bill heard the pew crack. He heard her sigh. Now she is hurt, he thought. I could swat her.

"Yes," Bill said, more softly now. "It is possible for you to overcome this demon." He tried to think about what the basis of the jealousy might be.

"Without naming names," he said carefully, "tell me a little more about this, uh, demon."

"She seems to get all the attention all the time. Without really deserving it. I mean, she does nothing to help. I asked her to join the altar guild and she said no. When she came to church some time ago, which she rarely does, I might add, I asked her if she'd like to serve on the Episcopal Church Women's Committee, and she said no thank you, just like that."

"Yes," Bill interrupted. "But to get to your jealousy . . ."

"I am," Mrs. Stanley almost snapped. "She does almost nothing, as I said, but she gets so much attention. She always has paint on her fingers; she doesn't dress for church. She doesn't care to do her hair. She is never on time."

Bill sighed. The light had dawned.

"But, but," Mrs. Stanley said, "she gets attention. And I, I work so hard." A pause. "I work so hard, and do so much. Last week, I polished the coffee urn."

That hideous object. Bill thought he had hidden it perfectly in the sacristy, deep in the shelves that held the half-burned altar candles.

"Someone had put it in the wrong place," Mrs. Stanley went on, "and I had meant to polish it for weeks. So I brought in my Wright's silver cream and several clean cloths and then I had to look for it, high and low, until—you won't believe this—I found it in the sacristy."

"No!" Bill said.

"Yes," said Mrs. Stanley. "So I spent all morning polishing it with Wright's—that's the best silver polish—and then wrapping it back up in its special flannel and putting it away. All of Saturday morning!"

"But to get to the jealousy," Bill said again.

"Well, I am jealous," Mrs. Stanley said. "I am. I know it. And I shouldn't be. I mean, I have reason to be, but I shouldn't be. The little green monster, my mother always said. Why green?"

"I don't know," Bill said.

"Well, green, blue. I am. And it's between me and God. When I come to church I think about her rather than my prayers."

"Indeed," Bill said. Then he said, "Mrs. Stanley, I wonder if you would be interested in serving on the jumble sale planning committee? There are, of course, many meetings, and most of them with my poor self, but perhaps you would consider?"

"I would be delighted," she said, her breath racking in her lungs.

"Very good," Bill said. "And I would give the jealousy to Our Lord for Him to take and carry for you."

"Ah," wheezed Mrs. Stanley. "I will give it to Him. I will give it up to Him." Bill heard the soft wheeze of asthmatic weeping.

"Yes," Bill said. "Rest easy."

He stood, to signal that the confession was over, and waited for her to collect herself. He heard a rustle of clothing and handkerchief, a blowing of the nose. A final wheeze. Bill turned around. He saw, for a moment, a Mrs. Stanley not often seen, or at least a Mrs. Stanley he did not often see. Her face was altered. It was calm, relaxed; the tears had taken away the clenched jaw, the snapping, judgmental eyes, the haughty nose. Her brown eyes took him in. Some power was present in her still, plain body as she hoisted herself out of the pew. Bill reached out his hand and she took it. Even as she did, he saw the face beginning to change back into its former half-martyred, half-judging expression.

"Mrs. Stanley," he said. "I must say you look splendid today," and the face relaxed again and a little coquettish smile crinkled her mouth.

"Thank you," she said. "I have a new hairdresser."

"Well, whatever it is," Bill said, "you look fine. Go in peace."

She smiled and held his hand a second longer, then rustled her way out of the pew and down the side aisle. He watched her back. She turned at the door and waved. The sun was bright behind her. And then she was gone.

Bill walked toward the sacristy and looked up at the lit candle hanging near the altar as he passed. He bowed to it—he was always somewhat awkward when he did this, as if someone were watching—and moved into the sacristy itself. He heard two altar guild women talking inside. A giggle.

"I hear that Father Williams has, shall we say, been caught dipping his pen in the parish inkwell."

"Really?"

"I heard it from Rose Ballentine yesterday."

"No."

"Well, the woman in question is a divorcée." The voice was unmistakably Julia Grimes, the widow of a former rector of All Saints, a veteran gossip.

"I hope it's just rumor," said the other voice as Bill opened the creaking sacristy door with a bit more energy than necessary.

"Oh," Julia exclaimed. "Hello, Father Taylor. I didn't know you were here."

"Good morning, Julia," Bill said. "And Lou." She smiled. Bill liked Lou. She rarely gossiped.

The two women looked at him like two flowers gazing at the sun. Bill hoped his shirt didn't have a stain and that his collar was clean.

"We're getting ready for the service," Julia said, gazing lovingly at her own plump hands pulling the chalice from its felt cover.

"Isn't that a new ring I see?" Bill had said.

"Why, yes," Julia replied. "It is. My aunt sent it to me, a family piece."

"Very pretty. It becomes you," Bill lied. "Let me know if you need anything. I'll be in my office." And he rushed from the room as if he had important things to do.

Once inside his office, he looked out into the bare courtyard of the church, with its one Russian olive tree, thorned and silver-leafed. Soon June would be here; the summer would be in full bloom. The tourists would arrive from Texas; the children in the Sunday school would behave badly. In September, Fiesta and Zozobra, Old Man Gloom, with his long puppet arms and papier-mâché head, would be burned on the hill overlooking the town. He looked at his hands. His mind kept returning to Mrs. Stanley, to her need to place the object of her jealousy in a dim light. To blame Eleanor for failings, for tardiness, for paint on her fingers, but most of all for the attention given to her, unearned. To blame Eleanor for Mrs. Stanley's own resentment at her dutiful polishing of that hideous urn, her resentment while polishing also undigested, unseen, and thrown back at Eleanor, who did not need to polish urns to be noticed. To blame Eleanor for all that was inside Mrs. Stanley but too dark and disgusting—now there was a word—to admit. How could one admit to wanting attention? Or to polishing an urn to get it?

Jealousy, Bill thought. How often he had seen that sin in different disguises in his years as a priest. He remembered the man in New York, at his first parish, when he was a lowly curate, who used to complain about his son's "tightfistedness" as he made more and more money. With a bit of probing from Bill, it turned out that the young man had sent his father expensive gifts (one was a sterling silver cigarette case, as Bill remembered) on birthdays and Christmas, and made an offer to take him to London, but the tightfisted complaint remained in place. Gradually, as Bill listened to the man, he heard the source of it: the man was jealous of his son's wealth and his ability to be generous.

How could one admit, Bill thought, to wanting the attention of a parishioner who was, as yet, not giving it? How could one confess to being jealous of a man one had never met? A man, one might add, who had done nothing to deserve the attention he got while another man worked to care for her, listened, prayed, offered help—polishing, Bill thought wryly, polishing. And, perhaps worse, the self-righteousness of it. The way he had imagined he could rescue her from some dark lurking *thing*, when she herself had told him she did not need rescue, had decided against the need to speak of the man who had stayed in her house. And what to do now, with David suddenly demanding he make good on his promise. He looked out at the courtyard, and then at the clock. A knock at the door. Lou called through it, "Father Taylor, time for the service," and he jumped up, opened the door, and followed her into the sacristy, where he hastily put on an alb and his stole, and marched through the little door into the church, ringing the bell that hung just outside the doorway as he passed it, to his tiny assembly, for Friday-morning prayer.

TWENTY-TWO

After the Friday service was over, Bill walked slowly back to the rectory and was rearranging a few papers on his desk when he heard a rap on the door. Bill opened it and found David, as he knew he would, standing on his front step. He had never entertained David in his house before, and a silly social shyness overcame him in the midst of his far more awful dread and fear. He fell back on fussiness.

"Oh, David," he said. "What a surprise! Will you come in, have some coffee? A pastry?"

"Have you talked to your parishioner?" David said, barging into the room with tremendous speed and energy, as if he had been launched. He had large circles under his eyes.

"No," Bill said.

"Take me there," David said.

Bill stared at him. David took a few steps forward, his fists bunched. Bill took a step back. He felt the need for a drink and pictured with great clarity a highball glass, one of his father's thick crystal heavyweights with about two fingers of scotch.

He turned away from David, a slight pull of his shoulder, so that he was standing almost at an angle, as if to make himself thinner, or one-dimensional. To steady himself, he placed his hand on the hall table, where the newspaper was sitting next to the nested boxes of enameled birds that he had placed there last night. He prayed for something he could not name. Then he turned back, and as he moved, he felt as if everything were slowing down, as if the room were filling with honey. He was in the world and the world on its orbit was turning, a great balanced globe, all of it slowing, his hand on the table, the light on his hand. He wondered if he would faint, but he didn't feel faint. He felt as if he were swaying on board a ship but was getting used to it, as if acquiring sea legs.

David was glaring at him.

"No," Bill replied.

"What!" David said, stepping closer. "What do you mean, no!"

"I mean no," Bill said, his voice a thin squeak, the room still flowing slowly around him.

"Then I will tell them who she is and how she harbors him. And you, how you knew of him and didn't tell. National security," David whispered. "You could go to prison for many years. And she, too."

Bill prayed into the slowness.

Then both of them heard it, the knock on the door, and then the door opening.

"Father Bill?" she called out. "It's Eleanor."

David swiveled around, his hands bunched into fists. Bill started forward, toward the door, but David threw his arm out and it caught Bill across the chest.

"Father Bill?" she called again, and walked hesitantly into the room. As she saw David and Bill, she stopped.

"Eleanor," Bill said. "This is David Stein."

"Good afternoon," she said.

David turned to Bill. "Your parishioner," he said, a satisfied smile on his face.

"No, actually," Bill said. "Just a friend. From college. Ah, New York."

David looked at him with great pity. He then turned to Eleanor. "You have met a friend of mine," he said. "He and I work together. I would like to see him again."

Eleanor kept her mouth in a line. "I don't know what you are talking about," she said finally.

"It's simple, really," David said, moving toward her until he stood too close for comfort and she stepped back.

"I need to talk to him. If I don't find him, there will be hell to pay. For him, for you, and for"—and he turned toward the priest—"for Father Bill."

Eleanor felt herself shrinking inside. No one had ever threatened her. She wanted to fall down, to give him whatever he wanted. She said nothing.

Bill said, "David. That is enough. You will leave my house now. Or I will call the police."

David smiled at him. "I am sorry, Bill," he said. "But I am the police. Or, rather . . ." He pulled from his pocket a small badge, with a scrawled signature. He showed this to Eleanor. "The FBI."

She stepped back.

"We think Leo Kavan may be a spy," he continued. "He has been missing from our Project for almost two months. We have no idea who he has told of our affairs."

"Good Lord," Bill said.

"Where is he?" David said to Eleanor.

She looked at him, his large eyes and his hand holding the badge. She tried to hold on to the way she felt when she had stood in her house at night, singing to herself, the touch of Leo's hand on her wrist.

"I don't know," she replied.

"Lying to an agent is a federal offense," he said.

"She doesn't know," Bill said. "It has been a long time since he was at her house," and then thought, Oh, God, what have I said.

"When was he at your house?" David asked.

"I don't know," she said. "I found a man by the river, sometime in the spring. He was ill. He left after a few days."

"You are lying," David said. "Do you know what I can do to you?"

"No," she whispered, and fought the tears that began to run down her cheeks.

"Why don't you sit down," David commanded, pulling a chair close to Eleanor.

"No, thank you," she replied.

Bill moved over to her. He put an arm around her shoulder. "She doesn't know anything, David," he said.

"Take me to your house," David said to Eleanor.

Eleanor tried to calculate. Time, distance, speed. How far might they have gone?

"I need to visit the ladies' room," she said.

"That will just have to wait," David said, roughly taking her arm. "Let's go."

"Hold on," Bill said. "I'll come with you."

David looked at him. "Yes, you come, too," he said.

The three of them walked out into the sun. There were people on the street. A man was walking his dog, and a woman opened her gate across the street from the church. Eleanor couldn't understand how they were going about their lives.

"We'll take your car," David said. "I'll drive."

David handed Eleanor into the front passenger seat and opened the door for Bill in the back. He closed both doors and then walked around to the driver's side. As he got in, with a huff of breath, he reached over with his right hand, palm up, and held it in front of Eleanor. She rummaged in her purse for her keys.

"Come on!" David said.

Eleanor handed the keys to him and he started the engine.

They drove down Palace Avenue toward the plaza. Eleanor watched the familiar stores and houses passing by the car. There was the entrance to the Shed with its quaint hand-painted sign. She was sitting in a car next to an FBI agent, who was working with Leo on a . . . ?

What did he say, project? Her brain wasn't working. Everything felt fuzzy.

When they got to the edge of the plaza, she gestured with her hand to turn right. David headed the car toward Taos. As they passed the post office, Eleanor thought she might scream, and a strange giggle came out of her throat. David looked over.

"Don't go nuts on me," he said.

Bill patted her shoulder from the back seat. She reached across her chest and touched his hand.

"Don't you take me on a wild goose chase," David said.

"Oh, no," Eleanor said. "I wouldn't."

As they drove out onto the highway, past the pinions and the yellow rabbit brush, she looked up at the Sangre de Cristos and said a prayer that Griefa and Leo might have made the turn in the road that would put them out of sight. Please, she said to herself. Give them a few minutes.

They passed Buckman Road, leading off to the left, and Eleanor kept silent. But after a few miles, David slowed the car.

"You live by the river," he said. "That road leads there."

Eleanor said nothing.

David spun around on the highway and headed south. At Buckman, he took the turn too fast, skidded, and nearly slid off the road. Eleanor pushed her fist into her mouth. The engine died.

Good, Eleanor thought.

David started up again, jammed the gears, and swerved back onto the road.

"No monkey business," he said.

"Oh, no," Eleanor replied.

They were on the flats now; blue asters were blooming along the roadside, the sage stretched toward the Jemez to the west. Eleanor could see Black Mesa off in the distance. She felt cold, as if her bones were freezing inside her. A roadrunner crossed the road in front of them, and Eleanor closed her eyes. When she opened them, the bird had made it to the other side. She looked over at David, who was driving hunched over the wheel, peering at the road ahead. When she looked back, she saw them, two figures sitting on a cart drawn by a horse, just making the turn off Buckman and heading south. She stared straight ahead.

If they had left only two minutes later, he would have been home free. Two more minutes of time, and the cart would have completed the turn at Sandia Road and been out of sight, and she would have taken David Stein on the wild goose chase she had planned for him. But as it was, it was not two minutes later.

The car bore down on the cart. Eleanor said nothing. Her hands were cold in her lap. When they came abreast of the cart, David slowed, rolled down the window, and peered out. Eleanor willed the car to continue.

She saw Leo glance over at the car, and how his face changed when he saw first David and then her.

David pulled in front of the cart, got out, and walked back.

"Dr. Kavan," he said, looking up at Leo sitting on the seat.

Griefa sat silent, holding the reins.

"We meet again."

"Good afternoon, Mr. Stein," Leo said, getting down from the cart.

"Where have you been? We have missed you."

"Camping," Leo replied.

"So it seems. But it's been a long camping trip. Isn't it time you rejoined us?"

"I am on my way to Chicago just now," Leo said. "And it isn't really any business of yours, anyway."

"Oh," said David, pulling out his badge. "But it is."

Leo peered at it. "What is that?"

"FBI," David said. "Surely you know what this is. Surely you, an enemy alien, know what this is."

"I have no way of knowing if that is a real, uh, credential," Leo said, noticing that his hand shook as he put it through his hair. But he knew that David was indeed what he said he was. It answered the question, at the back of his mind all day, of how it was that David Stein, a mere mechanist, had played chess every week with a minister when no one from the Project was allowed to talk to civilians on the streets of Santa Fe.

"That's true, Dr. Kavan. We will just have to go together back to the Hill, and then we can find out. Or you could tell me now what you know about the test of the gadget. Where it might be, for example."

Eleanor was shaking. She got out of the car and ran to Leo, who put his arm around her. He felt her body next to his, smelled the scent of her hair.

"Mr. Stein," Leo said. "You have your job to do. I have mine. I need to go to Chicago, to talk to them about the gadget. I am not, as you well know, a spy."

"That is unfortunately not something we know. After the accident, you left without permission. You did not sign the very reasonable request given you by General Groves. You have stayed away with no explanation. You have sent two letters from the post office in Santa Fe. These things, you know, add up."

Leo felt sweat on his palms. "One of the letters, as you probably already know, was sent to Justice Felix Frankfurter, for President Roosevelt, and the second, for my boss at the Met Lab. To tell him I was coming. I have nothing to hide from you."

"About the test," David said.

Leo looked carefully at him. Why did he want to know?

"Somewhere in the south, I imagine," Leo said, feeling as if he had left his body somewhere up the road. How did it happen that he was here, talking to David Stein beside a horse cart? "I wasn't told."

David stepped closer to him. "What makes you think I believe that?"

Leo folded his arms across his chest. Why was this so important to David? Then he saw it, all of a piece. David, the game of murder, his easy lie. Two spies in one, Leo thought. What was it? Two birds for the cost of one? No, that wasn't it. His mind was muddled.

"David, I don't know where the test will be. The director had not told me by the time I left."

Eleanor leaned against Leo, watching David. She could feel Leo's body tense through his shirt. She tried to convey her love for him through her skin, her shirt, his shirt, and his skin. As if willing molecules to pass through all the cells of all the obstacles in between them.

David watched them. He remembered his wife, Naomi, in their little apartment, when he, dirty and tired after the long drive to Albuquerque, walked in the door, and how she rose to greet him, her lips opening with his name on them.

He looked over their shoulders that were placed together like two horses pulling the same cart, at the dark purple volcanic cones that rose up from the desert floor south of Santa Fe. He knew Leo Kavan was just exactly who he said he was. A physicist who had lost his taste for the result of his imagination. A man running to catch up. He would not be successful, David knew. He would run and run, but the thing he had envisioned would outstrip him. It was the nature of things. Still, it was something to witness—a man who desired to change history, to call things back from the bright light of human enterprise to the half-dark of human humility.

Maybe I've lost my taste for my own enterprise, David thought. And the love they had for each other. He understood that.

"Go," he said suddenly. "Before I change my mind. You have a train to catch."

TWENTY-THREE

On Saturday morning, Bill was drinking coffee in the kitchen when he looked up and saw the two men in suits and slouch hats entering the courtyard between the rectory and the church. They seemed nonchalant, as if casting about for a lost Sunday paper or a dime. One was taller than the other and had a cowlick at the front of his blond hair. Bill almost snickered when he saw them, such obvious G-men.

But he didn't laugh when he heard them knock. He opened the door and they pushed inside. One minute they were outside and the next they were in. Cowlick led the way to the kitchen, where they stood, holding their hats. Bill, ever polite, offered them coffee. They refused. Their arms were folded in front of their chests. Cowlick untucked his hand and placed it firmly on Bill's arm.

"We are here to take a look around your house," he said.

"My house?" Bill said, his voice cracking. "Why?"

"It's war-related, Reverend Taylor," Cowlick said. "Just step out of the way, please."

Then they both turned and left the room.

Bill held himself still at the kitchen counter that had on it a dinner plate from last night and a dirty cup. He wished he had cleaned up. He wondered what one does when G-men are searching one's house. He could hear them, one in his private office and one in his bedroom, sounds of things rustling, a thud as a book or something heavier hit the floor. His house! Bill felt as if someone were taking off his clothes, one piece at a time. He stepped into the bedroom and saw Cowlick with his back to him, removing his clothes from the closet, throwing them onto the bed. A white dress shirt that he had not worn since he left the East—when? He felt that he had to remember precisely—just when had he worn it last? With his aunt at Victor's? The man pulled his clerical shirts out of the closet, letting them fall to the floor. Bill's hand had ironed each one. He stepped forward and tried to pick them up.

Through the window he saw the other man squatted down, digging in his vegetable garden. He walked quickly to the back door and called out to him, "Please, don't disturb the chile plants." Then he heard himself giggle, a guffaw. The G-man looked up at him, a frown of condescension, irritation, and then he slowly turned and addressed the Hatch red chile, nurtured and composted, that the Royce family had given Bill, a lifetime ago. His hand went around its stem and Bill lurched forward. The G-man ripped it out of the bed and then turned to Bill and smirked.

"Sorry," he said.

At the edge of his vision, Bill saw Mrs. Stanley standing outside the parish offices. It must be her day to volunteer to answer the phones, he thought vaguely. She was right on the threshold, and Bill wished she would wave or come over and greet him.

"Come inside," the man said roughly to Bill, pushing him toward the house, and Bill saw Mrs. Stanley step forward as if to help him, and then, as if in slow motion, step back.

Inside, Cowlick stood at his desk, reading a piece of paper, which Bill saw, walking forward, was a draft of his sermon for Sunday. He lunged forward, and the other man, now behind him, clasped a hand on his back.

"Easy, guy. No fast moves."

"My work," Bill said. "What is this about?"

"Sit down," the G-man said, as Cowlick turned.

"Reverend Taylor, we need your help," Cowlick began.

Bill looked at him.

"We need your help in a war-related matter."

That night Bill sat as the light dropped down, and the brilliant sunset turned the white wall of his study a pale translucent red. To calm his fear, he thought of how sin worked in a life, and he prayed for Eleanor and the man beside her, and for himself, and finally for David. And for the world as it was made.

TWENTY-FOUR

In the early light of high summer, the bus with the half-days wound up the long mountain road. David watched them get off the bus in a long file of calico skirts and dark bent heads. One of them jostled the other and laughed.

He walked to S-site, past the houses with the bathtubs. Oppenheimer had gone. Kitty was standing in the garden, picking snapdragons. Next to her was her little, quiet boy, Peter. David walked past. They did not wave.

Kistiakowsky was already at the site, inspecting the castings and sorting them into piles, one pile for the test, David knew, the other for the rejects, going to the Chinese copy. David surveyed the varnished brown pile. Each piece had been x-rayed and numbered. He was sweating through his shirt, his armpits damp. He swallowed, a dry throat.

Earlier, he and Kistiakowsky had plated the two hemispheres of the plutonium core with nickel. It shone beautifully, Kistiakowsky said, but the nickel blistered, ruining the fit. David had filed down the spheres, working late into the night as Kistiakowsky swore and paced. David smoothed the surfaces with gold foil. When Kistiakowsky saw the finished globe, he laughed. "Dressed in finery," he had said. "Silver and gold."

Kistiakowsky gestured toward the pile.

"For you, Davey," he said. "Wrap them like Christmas presents."

David and two other machinists assembled the unit in silence, packing the molds, snugging them with Kleenex and Scotch tape, at the slow pace of men exhausted by work and heat. Each mold was worth a fortune and could not fail.

Then David covered the assembly in waterproof plastic, boxed it in a shipping crate of pine boards, and secured it in the back of an army truck.

As David lashed a tarp over it all, Kistiakowsky watched him and shook his head. Something about that one, he had said to Frisch last night.

The shiny core left in the afternoon, shock-mounted in a field carrying case held by Morrison, who wore a summer suit of pale blue seersucker and sat upright in the back seat of an olive-colored army car. A car filled with guards drove out the gates in front of him, assembly specialists riding in another car behind him.

That night, just after midnight, Kistiakowsky got into one of the trucks carrying the assembly. It was Friday, the thirteenth of July. Kistiakowsky chose the day to thumb his nose at superstition.

David stood alone in the street as the last trucks drove out toward the gates. The moon rose late; its glittering path shone on the gravel between the trees, lighting up the mountains. It was so bright, David thought he had gone mad for a second, that the sun was shining at night.

3

August

TWENTY-FIVE

L eo had sat on the train to Chicago, awake for three days, as if keeping watch for her. Cornfields passed, silos, a man on horseback, a green pheasant in the grass. When he got to the city, he staggered from the train and found his way to a hotel, where he had slept for ten hours.

Then he had risen from the bed in the humidity, the force of which he had forgotten, and scribbled down the words of petitions that had been in his head. "Mr. Secretary of War: The military advantage and the saving of American lives that might result from using the atomic bomb against Japan may be outweighed . . ."

The next day, he took a cab to the Met Lab and to the director's dim office. His absence from Los Alamos was noted, the director said, his hands on the desk, a ring on the left hand. He had received Leo's letter from Santa Fe and had been waiting for him to arrive. Leo described his need to reflect on his work after Slotin's accident and the terrible pace. After a rest—and it was here that he stopped speaking for a brief time and the director looked hard at him. After a rest, Leo continued, he had come back here, to his old lab, to try to do what he could to change the course of history. As he said the word *history,* he saw it, not so much as a wave or tide inexorably going out or coming in, but as a stream of water finding the easiest channel, cutting through the mounds of mud he made as a child.

Men simply follow the way events are leaning, Leo thought that day. This is history.

He was glad to be back in a city, with its feeling of density, architecture, things made by human hands. He liked the feel of the thick morning newspaper rather than the broadsheet he'd been reading in Los Alamos. Old friends in the lab greeted him warmly, but he could see, too, the curiosity in their eyes, wariness. During a visit to a doctor in Chicago, he tried to tell him, without telling him, what had happened. The man was elderly, thoughtful, and recommended iron pills.

He walked on the Midway, the World's Fair walkway south of the university, muttering to himself. He worked every connection he could think of to find a way into the new administration. Truman was from Kansas City, Missouri; surely there must be someone from Missouri in the Met Lab. He discovered a mathematician, Albert Cohn, who had worked for the political machine in Kansas to get through graduate school. Cohn sent Leo's letter to his old boiler room boss. Three days after it arrived, Leo had an appointment at the State Department with Truman's new secretary of state.

He spent two sleepless nights walking the floor, preparing his speech. He felt he had one chance. He did not know much about the man he was to see, except that Truman trusted him. James Byrnes, from the American South. If he was the new secretary of state, he must be a learned, sophisticated man, Leo thought, a man used to thinking about the whole of the world, relationships among nations. He planned to talk to him about the larger picture he had seen, an arms race with Russia that would ruin both countries and make the world dangerous beyond measure. He asked Professor Einstein for a letter of introduction and got one: "I have much confidence in Dr. Kavan's judgment."

He wrote out a memorandum that ran to ten pages.

"Perhaps the greatest danger which faces us is the probability that our 'demonstration' of atomic bombs will precipitate a race in the production of these devices between the United States and Russia.

"This situation can be evaluated only by men who have firsthand knowledge of the facts involved, that is, by the small group of scientists who are actively engaged in this work."

He packed his bags, locked them, and took a train to the nation's capital. He got off into the heat of high summer in Washington, as if stepping into a laundry.

Byrnes's office was a large gracious suite with wallpaper of dark red, many desks and papers, a thick blue carpet that held Leo's shoes as he walked across it. Byrnes rose from his desk at the very last minute and reached across it to shake Leo's hand. He had a foxlike narrow face, with a pointed chin and large ears. He wore a sly schoolboy's expression. His suit was hand-tailored.

Byrnes offered coffee. Leo accepted. A black servant arrived a few minutes later carrying a heavy silver tray. He poured the men two cups, and Byrnes waved him away with his left hand while snapping open a cigarette case with his right. Leo gave him the Einstein letter and his memorandum.

While Byrnes glanced through the papers, Leo took a sip of coffee. It burned his mouth and he gagged. Byrnes's thin lips smiled. "Too hot?" He finished reading, smoothed his hands across the paper, and looked up at Leo.

"Mr. Secretary," Leo said, "I have come, as you know, to urge you to speak to the president about our use of the atomic bomb against Japan."

Byrnes sat back in his chair. "I have the greatest regard for you, Dr. Kavan," he said. "I understand you have been tireless in your work on our country's behalf. What is your native country? Poland? A proud nation."

Leo shifted in his chair. "Czechoslovakia, Mr. Secretary."

"What's that? Oh, of course."

"Perhaps the greatest immediate danger which faces us," Leo said, "is the probability that our use of atomic bombs will precipitate a race in the production of these devices between the United States and Russia."

Byrnes laughed. "General Groves tells me there is no uranium in Russia."

Leo, dumbfounded, said bluntly, "I am afraid that isn't true." Then he realized the mistake. Painstakingly, he explained, the way he used to explain a math lesson to a younger colleague: "General Groves must be speaking of radium extraction, for which one requires a high-grade ore, but for uranium, one may settle for low grade, which the Soviet Union undoubtedly has in abundance."

Byrnes pursed his lips and looked at his watch.

Leo felt himself sweating in the sweltering office, a fan's breeze hardly making a stir. He tried another tack: "It would be unwise to drop this bomb, because it would disclose that such a weapon existed."

Byrnes snorted. "We have spent two billion dollars on developing the bomb, and Congress will want to know what we got for the money spent. How would you get Congress to appropriate money for atomic energy research after the war is over if you do not show results for the money which has been spent already?" He placed his hands on his desk and made to stand up. "Tell me, Dr. Kavan, are your people safe in Hungary?"

"I beg your pardon, Mr. Secretary?"

"Your people. Your relatives. I fear for the Jewish people."

Leo stared at him. Byrnes stood up.

"Thank you for coming, Dr. Kavan. Your efforts on behalf of this country are laudable."

A thin young secretary with a flame of red hair appeared at Leo's side.

"Ah, Miss Keating. Would you show Dr. Kavan out? These hallways can be so confusing. Have a fine time in our capital, Dr. Kavan. Stop by the Lincoln Memorial if you have the time." Byrnes studied his desk.

Leo tried to speak, and the woman glided closer and gently took his elbow. He pulled his arm away and said to Byrnes, "Mr. Secretary, it may be very difficult to convince the world that a nation which was capable of secretly preparing and suddenly releasing a weapon as indiscriminate as the German rocket bomb and a million times more destructive is to be trusted in the future."

Byrnes looked up. His face was quizzical. "We should probably not speak of these things just now," he said, gesturing to the young woman. "If you take a left outside, you can pick up a taxi. Ask the driver how to get to the memorial. He will be happy to oblige." The woman took Leo's arm again, more firmly, and he turned toward her. She had an earnest freckled face, and wore red lipstick.

"One more thing," he said, looking back at the secretary. "May I urge you to take care in selecting the target. I understand there are American prisoners near some of the Japanese cities."

Byrnes frowned. "That is quite enough, Dr. Kavan," he said, and sat down at his desk. Miss Keating now pulled at him, and he walked with her through the dense carpet and out the door.

On the train home, he opened a news magazine and saw a series of photos.

"A Jap Burns" was the headline.

American soldiers had found Japanese soldiers hidden in caves on

Borneo, the reporter said. Some had surrendered, but others refused. The Australians used flamethrowers to force them out.

Leo held the magazine closer; the photos were hard to see. The first was of a soldier wearing a helmet holding what looked like a large rifle with a blast of fire coming out of its nozzle. The second photograph was of a blackened thing engulfed in flames. A man, Leo made out, finally, a man with flames shooting out of his back and head. There were six photos in all. Someone had snapped pictures, Leo thought, sickened, of a human being on fire trying to escape. "Blind, still burning," the caption read. "He tries to crawl."

The reporter said that as long as the Jap refused to come out of his holes, "this was the only way."

Leo put the magazine down on his lap. He saw what he had not seen before.

When he got to Chicago, he found a message from a friend who had been in high-level meetings in Washington. They met at the Coq d'Or at the Drake.

The man sipped scotch from a heavy clear glass and took a bunch of salted nuts in his left hand.

"You can't stop it, Leo," he said. "There is no institution, no group of citizens in opposition. And nothing can be organized, because it is a secret."

"We could be," Leo had said. "Those of us here in the lab. We can organize, because we are the ones who know."

"Listen, Leo," the man said, leaning close to him. "They have intercepted Japanese coded cables, including one between the emperor of Japan and his envoy in Moscow. The Japs are exploring conditional surrender."

"Thank God," Leo said.

"Besides," his friend went on, "Stalin will be in the Jap war before August fifteenth. *Fini* Japs when that comes about."

Leo went back to his hotel and drafted another petition, which he circulated in Chicago and then sent to Oak Ridge. It urged President Truman not to use atomic weapons against Japan "unless the terms which will be imposed upon Japan have been made public in detail and Japan, knowing these terms, has refused to surrender." By the end of two weeks, he had gathered one hundred and fifty-five Manhattan Project signatures.

The following week, his friend called him again.

"They are choosing targets not previously damaged by air raids," he said to Leo in the bar at the Drake.

"But I thought the Japanese were ready to surrender!"

"Not unconditionally, it seems. Unconditional surrender is what we want."

"But what does it matter?" Leo replied.

"Leo," his friend said quietly, "they want to use the gadget. They want to show the Russians who is boss."

Leo fell silent.

"Tokyo has been ruined by the firebombing," his friend went on, counting on his fingers. "They've made a list: Tokyo Bay, Yokohama, Nagoya, Osaka, Kobe, Hiroshima, Kokura, Fukuoka, Nagasaki, and Sasebo. They want an urban industrial site, preferably with weapons factories. It will probably depend on the weather. "

"There are prisoner-of-war camps near cities in Japan," Leo said. "How will they know where they are?"

His friend looked at him carefully. "Reconnaissance," he said.

"Notoriously unreliable," Leo said, wiping his forehead.

"Since when are you worried about American prisoners?"

"A woman I know. Her brother."

His friend looked at him sharply. "It can't be stopped, Leo," he said. "You are a scientist and you believe that it is good to find out how the world works."

"I used to believe that," Leo said. Then, "Now I think that the Americans must not use this bomb. It would be a crime against humanity."

The man put his fingers to his lips. "They will use it."

Leo nodded. Then he said, "Listen. This is only the beginning."

He had walked back to his hotel in the early August heat through the streets, twin aches in his heart.

At the hotel, a clerk with a scrubbed red face handed him a letter, forwarded from Box 1616. It was from the International Red Cross. Leo opened it and read, then sat down in the chair next to the desk and buried his face in his hands. The clerk bent down, touched his arm. Leo looked up at him, his face wet, and cried out: *"Mein die Schwester!"*

The clerk backed away, his lip curling. Leo staggered out of his chair and up the stairs to his room.

TWENTY-SIX

Bill stepped outside his new house, a squat four-room adobe at Otowi Bridge, at the base of the mountains just across the Rio Grande from the pueblo at San Ildefonso. The job was a good one, and he had been lucky to find it. The narrow-gauge railroad that ran north from Santa Fe to Antonito in Colorado had a small station here, in an old railroad boxcar, where freight and mail were unloaded a few times a week for the small communities near the river. Bill's job was to guard the various letters, packages, and kegs of nails until they were picked up. He also sold gas from an ancient and surly pump, and ran a small store out of the living room where he sold mainly Cokes and tobacco. It was enough to do, and there was still time left over to cultivate vegetables and patch up the house—when he had first arrived, holes in the floor were partially covered with pieces of tin, and an elderly chicken was roosting in the kitchen.

The quiet of the canyon behind the house and the rush of water in the river as it narrowed between rock walls below the bridge soothed him. On the days when the heavy, tarped military trucks crossed the bridge, heading either up the road leading to the old boys' school at Los Alamos or down it, he glanced up, startled by the noise.

The vestry had been quiet when Bill walked into the small parish library. He had glanced from one to the other of their clean faces, but not one of the men met his eye. They nodded to him—a sea of nods—and looked away. When the FBI questions a priest, it is best to part company, the senior warden had said to him the day before. He must think of the church. It was for the better.

What he missed even more than celebrating the Eucharist was preparing for it. Standing alone in the sacristy, waiting in the silence before walking through the door. Not knowing what it would be like, but ready. As a priest, when celebrating at least, he had been taught that he was a sort of flawed conduit for grace, but now he saw it reversed: the grace had flowed into him because he had needed it.

As the G-men questioned him, Bill had understood that it was David they were after. David, not Eleanor or Leo Kavan. Why the men were seeking information on a colleague he had not dared to ask.

He had told them that he and David played chess, once, sometimes twice a week. And David had said his work was related to the war. Of the events on the road leading to the train station at Lamy he had not spoken, thinking of them as privileged, that word used to describe a confession that he had thought of as only another word for "secret" but now understood as a rare and specific gift.

Every day, it seemed, he was redefining words he had thought he understood. *Privilege* and *destiny* and *faith* itself. Perhaps he would stay at Otowi Bridge long enough to understand how he had mistaken one word for another. He had very nearly cost a man his freedom— only love had intervened, in the last person he had thought capable of it. And as for Eleanor, on his better days he thought he had almost ruined her life, and on the worse ones he figured he had. How he had wished the best for her! How he had thought he knew what the best for her was.

He prayed, but not as he had used to. He realized that he had once prayed as if sending a memorandum to God: pay attention to this, and this, and that. Thank you for that and this. At the end, with the "amen," a perfunctory goodbye. Now he woke up in the morning and thought of the line in Matthew about laying up one's treasure where neither moth nor rust could consume it. He was inhabiting a world of moths and rust. Not to mention chickens and dirt and holes in the floor. The men and women who came to pick up their small packages and letters were just this side of moth-eaten, and they were often rusty with poverty and age. He wondered about whether he wanted to lay up his treasure in heaven or in this beautiful, passing world. He threw a worm on a hook into a nearby stream, and when he brought up a rainbow trout, the sight of it caused him almost to cry.

It was hot. The fifth of August. He looked forward to the fiesta coming soon when Zozobra, Old Man Gloom, would be burned.

TWENTY-SEVEN

Eleanor drew fine lines in pencil on a page of drawing paper until she had filled a rectangular sheet. She then washed the drawing with pale blue watercolor. She drew another and washed this one with yellow. The lines were horizontal, not vertical as in her paintings before now. They stopped just short of the edge. It was as if she had tipped her horizon, tilted the world. She felt she was entering Kandinsky's *Point and Line to Plane,* a geometry of near perfection.

The day before, she had driven into town to the post office in what had become a hopeless ritual and had seen inside her box a pale green letter. She turned her key in the lock and opened it. The envelope was marked with Japanese symbols, had two stamps with the emperor's face on them and the scrawled signature of a person affiliated with the Red Cross.

"Theodore Garrigue alive in hospital," the note read. He had been transferred to a new prison camp, the location of which could not be named. Somewhere in the Japanese chain of islands, the Red Cross surmised. They were scattered all over, the Red Cross told her, camps with white soldiers starving. He was receiving treatment for malaria. That was all. It was dated July 15.

She stood in the post office with tears running down her face, the letter clutched in her right hand. The same hand with which she would make her pale drawings.

She wrote back telling him to hold on. She filled the letter with memories. She reminded him of the lake, and the day he lay on his back in the rowboat. Sis hemming his pants in the large kitchen with the pots hanging overhead, Cook making French toast at the stove. The long table that looked out on birch trees and the rolling lawn. The string of wild turkeys who wandered past on Thanksgiving Day. The boathouse groaning against the tide. Sent to clean the boathouse by Father, they found that otters had been living under the guide boat that was upturned on rollers. She mailed her letter and prayed for him all the way home.

Knowing he was alive made her fear greater. She realized she had numbed herself. And so she began the drawings. They required her full attention. They were the same size as the letter about Teddy, and they were made in pencil. The drawings were records, traces, footprints. They contained the color of some new beginning, and they could be erased.

She had driven home from the train station holding the steering wheel with both hands, the windows rolled down to let in the dust and heat. She wanted to feel the desert around her. They had stood in line for tickets like a husband and wife, but when they got to the window where the clerk sat wearing a striped cap, Mr. Simms bought only one, one way. She had stepped onto the train with him, kissed him on the mouth, and stepped off; his hand held hers until the train chugged them apart.

As she drove, she took the hand he had held and kissed the palm.

When she had returned home, she found a batch of tamales covered in a white cloth that Griefa had left on the stove.

Eleanor lay awake that night, her body aching for Leo. In the morning, she got up and walked with Rita into the arroyo, where she sat in the sun, sifting gravel in her hand while the dog sniffed the air. Then she returned to the house and wrote Edgar a letter.

I am planning to stay here this year, she wrote. I will not be coming back to New York. She felt the unhooking of herself from him, like the sharp pain at the removal of stitches. In the end, her understanding of her marriage felt to her as if she had been driving on the road to Dusty, as she had when she had first arrived in New Mexico, with her windows fogged up, only a little patch clear enough through which to see. Gradually, as happens on a windshield, other little patches had cleared so the road ahead became easier to see, but only in fragments, until at one moment, as if by magic, the whole of it was clear and one could see all that was needed. I loved you, she wrote, now I know.

The end of the war with Germany had eased gasoline restrictions, so she drove out into the country again and returned to the chapels and churches in the north, praying for Teddy, and now for Leo, too. On the way home, she stopped sometimes at the house at Otowi Bridge where Bill lived now and they sat on his *portal* and watched the river coursing into the canyon. He had tried one day to ask her forgiveness.

"Eleanor," he said. "I am so sorry about what I did. I cannot tell you."

She put a hand on his arm and then withdrew it.

"I didn't understand," she said. "I didn't think of you as human."

Their gaze returned to the river. It was as if they were waiting.

She stood up from a pencil drawing to stretch. It was a hot day in early August.

TWENTY-EIGHT

August 6, 1945

Eleanor woke up early that morning. She got up to close the windows to hold some of the night's cool air inside the house during the hot day to come. She padded into her kitchen area to make coffee, turning on the radio as she passed to hear the early morning news.

Leo had been out walking late and was sound asleep when Cohn pounded on his door. He did not know where he was for a second, having dreamed of his home in Prague in great detail: the feel of the old staircase banister was still under his hand as he called out to ask who it was.

Bill made coffee that morning for the engineer who would be there on the early train. He saw it coming up the tracks toward him, and the engineer leaning out his cab, waving a red kerchief. Bill waved back, surprised, as the man was a quiet fellow who rarely spoke.

David heard the news over the Los Alamos PA system: "Attention please, attention please: one of our units has been successfully dropped on Japan."

They gathered in the auditorium, and Oppenheimer strode up the aisle, shaking hands as he went. When he got to the stage, he raised his fists in an awkward victory salute.

He told them what General Groves had said on the telephone:
"I'm proud of you and all your people."

"It went all right?" Oppenheimer had asked.

"Apparently it went with a tremendous bang," Groves said.

A great roar went up. Various men ran to the few phone lines and booked tables at La Fonda. Feynman drove a Jeep past the auditorium, and Laura Fermi hopped on the hood and rode it down the main street. The children charged through the streets of Los Alamos banging on pots and pans—an impromptu parade.

Eleanor's hand went to her mouth.

Leo fell to his knees in the hallway of the hotel.

Bill listened to the engineer talking excitedly about the secret project just up the hill from where they stood.

"An atomic bomb!" he said. "It wiped out a Jap city. One bomb!" And Bill saw the various mysteries—David, Leo, Eleanor—falling into place.

The man handed him the morning's *New Mexican* with the headline "Los Alamos Secret Disclosed by Truman" over the larger words "Atomic Bombs Drop on Japan."

"Hold on to this!" he said. "It'll be a keepsake for your grandchildren someday!"

Bill thanked him for the paper, helped with the mail sack, drew the engineer a cup of water from the well, and waved as the man climbed back up into the train's engine. Then he sat down on his *portal* and read the news. In the article, the city of Hiroshima was referred to as an army base. When he was finished, he looked up the road to the top of the hill. He imagined a city there, built overnight, where men like Leo and David had labored round the clock for the last two years. He wondered what that city looked like, and what the bomb itself, finally, resembled.

In all of the rumors, he had never imagined this. He walked over to his garden to pick summer squash from their sprawling vines, and as he worked, he pondered. He thought about Leo Kavan, and David, and whether he was what he said he was, a machinist and an FBI agent. And, Bill realized suddenly, what he had not said he was. That was why his colleagues had asked about him. So, in this enterprise with high stakes, there had been a spy after all. He wondered who David was spying for.

He placed the squash at the end of their rows, then loaded the yellow vegetables into a round apple basket. In the midst of the garden, he sat down on a warm patch of earth. He thought about David's choice on the road to Lamy. How Eleanor had helped Leo even as she didn't know enough. And, yes, his own decision not to tell David, in the end, how to find Leo, not that it had done much good.

On the day of reckoning, something he was not sure he believed in anymore, how would these frail things be weighed against the bomb's destruction? Bill thought of Abraham arguing with God over the destruction of Sodom and Gomorrah: If I find a hundred good men? Twenty? Ten? Would you stay your hand?

Three days later, after the second bomb was dropped on Nagasaki, Bill saw Eleanor's roadster speeding across the bridge.

As she walked toward him, he saw in her hand a yellow telegram. The tears were running down her face as she gave it to him. "Lt. Theodore Garrigue will be returning to the United States in a matter of weeks," the telegram read.

When he heard about Hiroshima, Teddy would tell her later, "I cried with relief and joy. We were going to live. We were going to grow old after all."

Bill and Eleanor sat together watching the river flowing by.

"I'm so glad Teddy is coming home," Bill said.

"Oh, sweet Jesus, so am I," she replied. "But, Bill."

"Yes," he said. "I know." He stopped. Then he went on. "Have you heard from . . ." He still had trouble saying the name. "Leo?"

"Yes," she said. "They found his sister. He is working on getting her here."

She did not speak of the rest of what he said. Or of her replies. She kept his letters in the same sandalwood box with those from Teddy.

"Bread from stones," he wrote to her. "You were that for me."

"And you for me," she wrote back.

TWENTY-NINE

In the lab on Long Island at Cold Spring Harbor, where Leo works now, he greets each day with a kind of genuflection. His health has held, for now, although he will never know for how long. He is glad to be alive. He studies only the smallest things, what is deeply old and still: pieces of bone caught in rock, microbes in ice. The mysteries of sea horses and algae, cell formation, the intricacies. A thing that changes and is infinite.

As he walks back to his house to greet Lotte and sit down to a meal she has made for him, he thinks of Eleanor. He remembers her wrist, and the stone of the silver bracelet, the fire burning late in the night. He remembers the smell of the room, the sweet pinion resin, the scent she wore. He thinks again of that universe that may run parallel to this one, or the many universes, and that in it she is walking in the door toward him, always, and he is opening his eyes to see her for the first time.

ACKNOWLEDGMENTS

I am indebted to the following authors and books: Richard Rhodes, *The Making of the Atomic Bomb*; Bernice Brode, *Tales of Los Alamos*; Robert Jungk, *Brighter than a Thousand Suns*; Otto Frisch, *What Little I Remember*; Frank Waters, *Masked Gods*; Marta Weigle, *Hispanic Villages of Northern New Mexico*; K.C. Cole, *Mind Over Matter*; Robert Serber, *The Los Alamos Primer*; Jane S. Wilson and Charlotte Serber, *Standing by and Making Do*; Peggy Pond Church, *The House at Otowi Bridge*; Ruben Cobos, *A Dictionary of New Mexico and Southern Colorado Spanish*; Charles Aranda, Dichos: *Proverbs and Sayings from the Spanish*.

I am also indebted to Jon Else for his film *The Day After Trinity*.

I thank Jodie Ireland, Peter Selgin, Helen Merrill, Richard Falk, Anne Makepeace, Sue Halpern, and Andra Lichtenstein for their support and encouragement. And Ellen Meloy, with us in spirit.

Thanks to Elisabeth Weber and Ann Finkbeiner for help with the final manuscript.

I thank Jane Garrett and Alexis Gargagliano at Knopf; Harriet Barlow and Ben Strader at the Blue Mountain Center; and the MacDowell Colony for early, crucial support.

My thanks to my astute, generous editor, Deb Garrison, and the team at Pantheon: Janice Goldklang, Caroline Zancan, Jenna Bagnini,

Elisabeth Calamari, Victoria Gerken, and Hillary Tisman. Thank you to Alison Kerr Miller for her careful copyedit.

I thank, always, my agent, Flip Brophy, and my goddaughter, Cia Glover.

And Vincent Stanley, sine quo non.

ALSO BY NORA GALLAGHER

THINGS SEEN AND UNSEEN
A Year Lived in Faith

Whether coping with her brother's battle against cancer, serving communion wine, or questioning the afterlife ("One world at a time"), Nora Gallagher draws us into a world of journeys and mysteries. By braiding together the symbols of the Christian calendar, the events of a year in the life of one church, and her own spiritual journey, Gallagher calls into focus "the world of the almost unknown" as she writes of faith and its meaning, of uncertainty and suffering, grace and commitment in this harrowingly honest memoir. Thought provoking and profoundly perceptive, *Things Seen and Unseen* is a remarkable demonstration that "the road to the sacred is paved with the ordinary."

Religion/Autobiography/978-0-679-77549-2

PRACTICING RESURRECTION
A Memoir of Work, Doubt, Discernment, and Moments of Grace

In her highly praised memoir, Nora Gallagher reflected on a year of spiritual renewal and the fact of mortality with uncommon wisdom and grace. We rejoin her in *Practicing Resurrection* as Gallagher searches for direction in the wake of her brother's death. A desire to reclaim her own "wild life" and a sense of the sacred in the world compels her to assess everything: her marriage, her writing career, and her commitment to parish life. A profound testimony to the urgency of living with meaning, to the natural world's solace and sacredness and a beautiful and often harrowing account of the search for vocation: Gallagher bears witness to the way death yields new life.

Religion/Spirituality/978-0-375-70563-2